ROALD

DAHL

LAMB TO THE SLAUGHTER AND OTHER STORIES

PENGUIN BOOKS

PENGUIN BOOKS

Published by the Penguin Group. Penguin Books Ltd, 27 Wrights Lane, London W8 5TZ, England. Penguin Books USA Inc., 375 Hudson Street, New York, New York 10014, USA. Penguin Books Australia Ltd, Ringwood, Victoria, Australia. Penguin Books Canada Ltd, 10 Alcorn Avenue, Toronto, Ontario, Canada M4V 3B2. Penguin Books (NZ) Ltd, 182–190 Wairau Road, Auckland 10, New Zealand · Penguin Books Ltd, Registered Offices: Harmondsworth, Middlesex, England · **These stories are taken from *The Collected Stories of Roald Dahl*, published by Penguin Books in 1992.** This edition published 1995 · Typeset by Datix International Limited, Bungay, Suffolk. Printed in England by Clays Ltd, St Ives plc · 10 9 8 7 6 5 4 3 2 1

CONTENTS

Parson's Pleasure

Mr Boggis was driving the car slowly, leaning back comfortably in the seat with one elbow resting on the sill of the open window. How beautiful the countryside, he thought; how pleasant to see a sign or two of summer once again. The primroses especially. And the hawthorn. The hawthorn was exploding white and pink and red along the hedges and the primroses were growing underneath in little clumps, and it was beautiful.

He took one hand off the wheel and lit himself a cigarette. The best thing now, he told himself, would be to make for the top of Brill Hill. He could see it about half a mile ahead. And that must be the village of Brill, that cluster of cottages among the trees right on the very summit. Excellent. Not many of his Sunday sections had a nice elevation like that to work from.

He drove up the hill and stopped the car just short of the summit on the outskirts of the village. Then he got out and looked around. Down below, the countryside was spread out before him like a huge green carpet. He could see for miles. It was perfect. He took a pad and pencil from his pocket, leaned against the back of the car, and allowed his practised eye to travel slowly over the landscape.

He could see one medium farmhouse over on the right, back in the fields, with a track leading to it from the road. There was another larger one beyond it. There was a house surrounded by tall elms that looked as though it might be a Queen Anne, and there were two likely farms away over on the left. Five places in all. That was about the lot in this direction.

Mr Boggis drew a rough sketch on his pad showing the position of each so that he'd be able to find them easily when he was down below, then he got back into the car and drove up through the village to the other side of the hill. From there he spotted six more possibles – five farms and one big white Georgian house. He studied the Georgian house through his binoculars. It had a clean prosperous look, and the garden was well ordered. That was a pity. He ruled it out immediately. There was no point in calling on the prosperous.

In this square then, in this section, there were ten possibles in all. Ten was a nice number, Mr Boggis told himself. Just the right amount for a leisurely afternoon's work. What time was it now? Twelve o'clock. He would have liked a pint of beer in the pub before he started, but on Sundays they didn't open until one. Very well, he would have it later. He glanced at the notes on his pad. He decided to take the Queen Anne first, the house with the elms. It had looked nicely dilapidated through the binoculars. The people there could probably do with some money. He was always lucky with Queen Annes, anyway. Mr Boggis climbed back into the car, released the handbrake, and began cruising slowly down the hill without the engine.

Apart from the fact that he was at this moment disguised in the uniform of a clergyman, there was nothing very sinister about Mr Cyril Boggis. By trade he was a dealer in antique furniture, with his own shop and showroom in the King's Road, Chelsea. His premises were not large, and generally he didn't do a great deal of business, but because he always bought cheap, very very cheap, and sold very very dear, he managed to make quite a tidy little income every year. He was a talented salesman, and when buying or selling a piece he could slide smoothly into whichever mood suited the client best. He could become grave and charming for the aged, obsequious for the rich, sober for the godly, masterful for the weak, mischievous for the widow, arch and saucy for the spinster. He was well aware of his gift, using it shamelessly on every possible occasion; and often, at the end of an unusually good performance, it was as much as he could do to prevent himself from turning aside and taking a bow or two as the thundering applause of the audience went rolling through the theatre.

In spite of this rather clownish quality of his, Mr Boggis was not a fool. In fact, it was said of him by some that he probably knew as much about French, English, and Italian furniture as anyone else in London. He also had surprisingly good taste, and he was quick to recognize and reject an ungraceful design, however genuine the article might be. His real love, naturally, was for the work of the great eighteenth-century English designers, Ince, Mayhew, Chippendale, Robert Adam, Manwaring, Inigo Jones, Hepplewhite, Kent, Johnson, George Smith, Lock, Sheraton, and the rest of them, but even with these he occasionally drew the line. He refused, for example, to allow a single piece from Chippendale's Chinese or Gothic period to come into his showroom, and the same was true of some of the heavier Italian designs of Robert Adam.

During the past few years, Mr Boggis had achieved considerable fame among his friends in the trade by his ability to produce unusual and often quite rare items with astonishing regularity. Apparently the man had a source of supply that was almost inexhaustible, a sort of private warehouse, and it seemed that all he had to do was to drive out to it once a week and help himself. Whenever they asked him where he got the stuff, he would smile knowingly and wink and murmur something about a little secret.

The idea behind Mr Boggis's little secret was a simple one, and it had come to him as a result of something that had happened on a certain Sunday afternoon nearly nine years before, while he was driving in the country.

He had gone out in the morning to visit his old mother, who lived in Sevenoaks, and on the way back the fanbelt on his car had broken, causing the engine to overheat and the water to boil away. He had got out of the car and walked to the nearest house, a smallish farm building about fifty yards off the road, and had asked the woman who answered the door if he could please have a jug of water.

While he was waiting for her to fetch it, he happened to glance in through the door to the living-room, and there, not five yards from where he was standing, he spotted something that made him so excited the sweat began to come out all over the top of his head. It was a large oak armchair of a type that he had only seen once before in his life. Each arm, as well as the panel at the back, was supported by a row of eight beautifully turned spindles. The back panel itself was decorated by an inlay of the most delicate floral design, and the head of a duck was carved to lie along half the length of either arm. Good God, he thought. This thing is late fifteenth century!

He poked his head in further through the door, and there, by heavens, was another of them on the other side of the fireplace!

He couldn't be sure, but two chairs like that must be worth at least a thousand pounds up in London. And oh, what beauties they were!

When the woman returned, Mr Boggis introduced himself and straight away asked if she would like to sell her chairs.

Dear me, she said. But why on earth should she want to sell her chairs?

No reason at all, except that he might be willing to give her a pretty nice price.

And how much would he give? They were definitely not for sale, but just out of curiosity, just for fun, you know, how much would he give?

Thirty-five pounds.

How much?

Thirty-five pounds.

Dear me, thirty-five pounds. Well, well, that was very interesting. She'd always thought they were valuable. They were very old. They were very comfortable too. She couldn't possibly do without them, not possibly. No, they were not for sale but thank you very much all the same.

They weren't really so very old, Mr Boggis told her, and they wouldn't be at all easy to sell, but it just happened that he had a client who rather liked that sort of thing. Maybe he could go up another two pounds – call it thirty-seven. How about that?

They bargained for half an hour, and of course in the end Mr Boggis got the chairs and agreed to pay her something less than a twentieth of their value.

That evening, driving back to London in his old station-wagon with the two fabulous chairs tucked away snugly in the back, Mr Boggis had suddenly been struck by what seemed to him to be a most remarkable idea.

Look here, he said. If there is good stuff in one farmhouse, then why not in others? Why shouldn't he search for it? Why shouldn't he comb the countryside? He could do it on Sundays. In that way, it wouldn't interfere with his work at all. He never knew what to do with his Sundays.

So Mr Boggis bought maps, large scale maps of all the counties around London, and with a fine pen he divided each of them up into a series of squares. Each of these squares covered an actual area of five miles by five, which was about as much territory, he estimated, as he could cope with on a single Sunday, were he to comb it thoroughly. He didn't want the towns and the villages. It was the comparatively isolated places, the large farmhouses and the rather dilapidated country mansions, that he was looking for; and in this way, if he did one square each Sunday, fifty-two squares a year, he would gradually cover every farm and every country house in the home counties.

But obviously there was a bit more to it than that. Country folk are a suspicious lot. So are the impoverished rich. You can't go about ringing their bells and expecting them to show you around their houses just for the asking, because they won't do it. That way you would never get beyond the front door. How then was he to gain admittance? Perhaps it would be best if he didn't let them know he was a dealer at all. He could be the telephone man, the plumber, the gas inspector. He could even be a clergyman . . .

From this point on, the whole scheme began to take on a more practical aspect. Mr Boggis ordered a large quantity of superior cards on which the following legend was engraved:

THE REVEREND
CYRIL WINNINGTON BOGGIS

President of the Society for the Preservation of Rare Furniture	*In association with The Victoria and Albert Museum*

From now on, every Sunday, he was going to be a nice old parson spending his holiday travelling around on a labour of love for the 'Society', compiling an inventory of the treasures that lay hidden in the country homes of England. And who in the world was going to kick him out when they heard that one?

Nobody.

And then, once he was inside, if he happened to spot something he really wanted, well – he knew a hundred different ways of dealing with that.

Rather to Mr Boggis's surprise, the scheme worked. In fact, the friendliness with which he was received in one house after another through the countryside was, in the beginning, quite embarrassing, even to him. A slice of cold pie, a glass of port, a cup of tea, a basket of plums, even a full sit-down Sunday dinner with the family, such things were constantly being pressed upon him. Sooner or later, of course, there had been some bad moments and a number of unpleasant incidents, but then nine years is more than four hundred Sundays, and that adds up to a great quantity of houses visited. All in all, it had been an interesting, exciting, and lucrative business.

And now it was another Sunday and Mr Boggis was operating in the country of Buckinghamshire, in one of the most northerly squares on his map, about ten miles from Oxford, and as he drove down the hill and headed for his first house, the dilapidated Queen Anne, he began to get the feeling that this was going to be one of his lucky days.

He parked the car about a hundred yards from the gates and got out to walk the rest of the way. He never liked people to see his car until after a deal was completed. A dear old clergyman and a large station-wagon somehow never seemed quite right together. Also the short walk gave him time to examine the property closely from the outside and to assume the mood most likely to be suitable for the occasion.

Mr Boggis strode briskly up the drive. He was a small

fat-legged man with a belly. The face was round and rosy, quite perfect for the part, and the two large brown eyes that bulged out at you from this rosy face gave an impression of gentle imbecility. He was dressed in a black suit with the usual parson's dog-collar round his neck, and on his head a soft black hat. He carried an old oak walking-stick which lent him, in his opinion, a rather rustic easy-going air.

He approached the front door and rang the bell. He heard the sound of footsteps in the hall and the door opened and suddenly there stood before him, or rather above him, a gigantic woman dressed in riding-breeches. Even through the smoke of her cigarette he could smell the powerful odour of stables and horse manure that clung about her.

'Yes?' she asked, looking at him suspiciously. 'What is it you want?'

Mr Boggis, who half expected her to whinny any moment, raised his hat, made a little bow, and handed her his card. 'I do apologize for bothering you,' he said, and then he waited, watching her face as she read the message.

'I don't understand,' she said, handing back the card. 'What is it you want?'

Mr Boggis explained about the Society for the Preservation of Rare Furniture.

'This wouldn't by any chance be something to do with the Socialist Party?' she asked, staring at him fiercely from under a pair of pale bushy brows.

From then on, it was easy. A Tory in riding-breeches, male or female, was always a sitting duck for Mr Boggis. He spent two minutes delivering an impassioned eulogy on the extreme Right Wing of the Conservative Party, then two more denouncing the Socialists. As a clincher, he made particular reference to the Bill that the Socialists had once introduced for the abolition of bloodsports in the country, and went on to inform his listener that his idea of heaven – 'though you better not tell the bishop, my dear' – was a place where one could hunt the fox, the stag, and the hare with large packs of tireless hounds from morn till night every day of the week, including Sundays.

Watching her as he spoke, he could see the magic beginning to do its work. The woman was grinning now, showing Mr Boggis a set of enormous, slightly yellow teeth. 'Madam,' he cried, 'I beg of you, *please* don't get me started on Socialism.' At that point, she let out a great guffaw of laughter, raised an enormous red hand, and slapped him so hard on the shoulder that he nearly went over.

'Come in!' she shouted. 'I don't know what the hell you want, but come on in!'

Unfortunately, and rather surprisingly, there was nothing of any value in the whole house, and Mr Boggis, who never wasted time on barren territory, soon made his excuses and took his leave. The whole visit had taken less than fifteen minutes, and that, he told himself as he climbed back into his car and started off for the next place, was exactly as it should be.

From now on, it was all farmhouses, and the nearest was about half a mile up the road. It was a large half-timbered brick building of considerable age, and there was a magnificent pear tree still in blossom covering almost the whole of the south wall.

Mr Boggis knocked on the door. He waited, but no one came. He knocked again, but still there was no answer, so he wandered around the back to look for the farmer among the cowsheds. There was no one there either. He guessed that they must all still be in church, so he began peering in the windows to see if he could spot anything interesting. There was nothing in the dining-room. Nothing in the library either. He tried the next window, the living-room, and there, right under his nose, in the little alcove that the window made, he saw a beautiful thing, a semicircular card-table in mahogany, richly veneered, and in the style of Hepplewhite, built around 1780.

'Ah-ha,' he said aloud, pressing his face hard against the glass. 'Well done, Boggis.'

But that was not all. There was a chair there as well, a single chair, and if he were not mistaken it was of an even finer quality than the table. Another Hepplewhite, wasn't it? And oh, what a beauty! The lattices on the back were finely carved with the honeysuckle, the husk, and the paterae, the caning on the seat was original, the legs were very gracefully turned and the two back ones had that peculiar outward splay that meant so much. It was an exquisite chair. 'Before this day is done,' Mr Boggis said softly, 'I shall have the pleasure of sitting down upon that lovely seat.' He never bought a chair without doing this. It was a favourite test of his, and it was always an intriguing sight to see him lowering himself delicately into the seat, waiting for the 'give', expertly gauging the precise but infinitesimal degree of shrinkage that the years had caused in the mortice and dovetail joints.

But there was no hurry, he told himself. He would return here later. He had the whole afternoon before him.

The next farm was situated some way back in the fields, and in order to keep his car out of sight, Mr Boggis had to leave it on the road and walk about six hundred yards along a straight track that led directly into the back yard of the farmhouse. This place, he noticed as he approached, was a good deal smaller than the last, and he didn't hold out much hope for it. It looked rambling and dirty, and some of the sheds were clearly in bad repair.

There were three men standing in a close group in a corner of the yard, and one of them had two large black greyhounds with him, on leashes. When the men caught sight of Mr Boggis walking forward in his black suit and parson's collar, they stopped talking and seemed suddenly to stiffen and freeze, becoming absolutely still, motionless, three faces turned towards him, watching him suspiciously as he approached.

The oldest of the three was a stumpy man with a wide frog-mouth and small shifty eyes, and although Mr Boggis didn't know it, his name was Rummins and he was the owner of the farm.

The tall youth beside him, who appeared to have something wrong with one eye, was Bert, the son of Rummins.

The shortish flat-faced man with a narrow corrugated brow and immensely broad shoulders was Claud. Claud had dropped in on Rummins in the hope of getting a piece of pork or ham out of him from the pig that had been killed the day before. Claud knew about the killing – the noise of it had carried far across the fields – and he also knew that a man should have a government permit to do that sort of thing, and that Rummins didn't have one.

'Good afternoon,' Mr Boggis said. 'Isn't it a lovely day?'

None of the three men moved. At that moment they were all thinking precisely the same thing – that somehow or other this clergyman, who was certainly not the local fellow, had been sent to poke his nose into their business and to report what he found to the government.

'What beautiful dogs,' Mr Boggis said. 'I must say I've never been greyhound-racing myself, but they tell me it's a fascinating sport.'

Again the silence, and Mr Boggis glanced quickly from

Rummins to Bert, then to Claud, then back again to Rummins, and he noticed that each of them had the same peculiar expression on his face, something between a jeer and a challenge, with a contemptuous curl to the mouth and a sneer around the nose.

'Might I inquire if you are the owner?' Mr Boggis asked, undaunted, addressing himself to Rummins.

'What is it you want?'

'I do apologize for troubling you, especially on a Sunday.'

Mr Boggis offered his card and Rummins took it and held it up close to his face. The other two didn't move, but their eyes swivelled over to one side, trying to see.

'And what exactly might you be wanting?' Rummins asked.

For the second time that morning, Mr Boggis explained at some length the aims and ideals of the Society for the Preservation of Rare Furniture.

'We don't have any,' Rummins told him when it was over. 'You're wasting your time.'

'Now, just a minute, sir,' Mr Boggis said, raising a finger. 'The last man who said that to me was an old farmer down in Sussex, and when he finally let me into his house, d'you know what I found? A dirty-looking old chair in the corner of the kitchen, and it turned out to be worth *four hundred pounds*! I showed him how to sell it, and he bought himself a new tractor with the money.'

'What on earth are you talking about?' Claud said. 'There ain't no chair in the world worth four hundred pound.'

'Excuse me,' Mr Boggis answered primly, 'but there are plenty of chairs in England worth more than twice that figure. And you know where they are? They're tucked away in the farms and cottages all over the country, with the owners using them as steps and ladders and standing on them with hobnailed boots to reach a pot of jam out of the top cupboard or to hang a picture. This is the truth I'm telling you, my friends.'

Rummins shifted uneasily on his feet. 'You mean to say all you want to do is go inside and stand there in the middle of the room and look around?'

'Exactly,' Mr Boggis said. He was at last beginning to sense what the trouble might be. 'I don't want to pry into your cupboards or into your larder. I just want to look at the furniture to see if you happen to have any treasures here, and then I can write about them in our Society magazine.'

'You know what I think?' Rummins said, fixing him with his small wicked eyes. 'I think you're after buying the stuff yourself. Why else would you be going to all this trouble?'

'Oh, dear me. I only wish I had the money. Of course, if I saw something that I took a great fancy to, and it wasn't beyond my means, I might be tempted to make an offer. But alas, that rarely happens.'

'Well,' Rummins said, 'I don't suppose there's any harm in your taking a look around if that's all you want.' He led the way across the yard to the back door of the farmhouse, and Mr Boggis followed him; so did the son Bert, and Claud with his two dogs. They went through the kitchen, where the only furniture was a cheap deal table with a dead chicken lying on it, and they emerged into a fairly large, exceedingly filthy living-room.

And there it was! Mr Boggis saw it at once, and he stopped dead in his tracks and gave a little shrill gasp of shock. Then he stood there for five, ten, fifteen seconds at least, staring like an idiot, unable to believe, not daring to believe what he saw before him. It *couldn't* be true, not possibly! But the longer he stared, the more true it began to seem. After all, there it was standing against the wall right in front of him, as real and as solid as the house itself. And who in the world could possibly make a mistake about a thing like that? Admittedly it was painted white, but that made not the slightest difference. Some idiot had done that. The paint could easily be stripped off. But good God! Just look at it! And in a place like this!

At this point, Mr Boggis became aware of the three men, Rummins, Bert, and Claud, standing together in a group over by the fireplace, watching him intently. They had seen him stop and gasp and stare, and they must have seen his face turning red, or maybe it was white, but in any event they had seen enough to spoil the whole goddamn business if he didn't do something about it quick. In a flash, Mr Boggis clapped one hand over his heart, staggered to the nearest chair, and collapsed into it, breathing heavily.

'What's the matter with you?' Claud asked.

'It's nothing,' he gasped. 'I'll be all right in a minute. Please – a glass of water. It's my heart.'

Bert fetched him the water, handed it to him, and stayed close beside him, staring down at him with a fatuous leer on his face.

'I thought maybe you were looking at something,' Rummins said. The wide frog-mouth widened a fraction further into a crafty grin, showing the stubs of several broken teeth.

'No, no,' Mr Boggis said. 'Oh dear me, no. It's just my heart. I'm so sorry. It happens every now and then. But it goes away quite quickly. I'll be all right in a couple of minutes.'

He *must* have time to think, he told himself. More important still, he must have time to compose himself thoroughly before he said another word. Take it gently, Boggis. And whatever you do, keep calm. These people may be ignorant, but they are not stupid. They are suspicious and wary and sly. And if it is really true – no it *can't* be, it *can't* be true . . .

He was holding one hand up over his eyes in a gesture of pain, and now, very carefully, secretly, he made a little crack between two of the fingers and peeked though.

Sure enough, the thing was still there, and on this occasion he took a good long look at it. Yes – he had been right the first time! There wasn't the slightest doubt about it! It was really unbelievable!

What he saw was a piece of furniture that any expert would have given almost anything to acquire. To a layman, it might not have appeared particularly impressive, especially when covered over as it was with dirty white paint, but to Mr Boggis it was a dealer's dream. He knew, as does every other dealer in Europe and America, that among the most celebrated and coveted examples of eighteenth-century English furniture in existence are the three famous pieces known as 'The Chippendale Commodes'. He knew their history backwards – that the first was 'discovered' in 1920, in a house at Moreton-in-Marsh, and was sold at Sotheby's the same year; that the other two turned up in the same auction rooms a year later, both coming out of Raynham Hall, Norfolk. They all fetched enormous prices. He couldn't quite remember the exact figure for the first one, or even the second, but he knew for certain that the last one to be sold had fetched thirty-nine hundred guineas. And that was in 1921! Today the same piece would surely be worth ten thousand pounds. Some man, Mr Boggis couldn't remember his name, had made a study of these commodes fairly recently and had proved that all three must have come from the same workshop, for the veneers were all from the same log, and the same set of templates had been used in the construction of each. No invoices had been found for any of them, but all the experts were agreed that these three commodes could have been executed only by Thomas Chippendale himself, with his own hands, at the most exalted period in his career.

And here, Mr Boggis kept telling himself as he peered cautiously through the crack in his fingers, here was the fourth Chippendale Commode! And *he* had found it! He would be rich! He would also be famous! Each of the other three was known throughout the furniture world by a special name – The Chastleton Commode, The First Raynham Commode, The Second Raynham Commode. This one would go down in history as The Boggis Commode! Just imagine the faces of the boys up there in London when they got a look at it tomorrow morning! And the luscious offers coming in from the big fellows over in the West End – Frank Partridge, Mallet, Jetley, and the rest of them! There would be a picture of it in *The Times*, and it would say, 'The very fine Chippendale Commode which was recently discovered by Mr Cyril Boggis, a London dealer . . .' Dear God, what a stir he was going to make!

This one here, Mr Boggis thought, was almost exactly similar to the Second Raynham Commode. (All three, the Chastleton and the two Raynhams, differed from one another in a number of small ways.) It was a most impressive handsome affair, built in the French rococo style of Chippendale's Directoire period, a kind of large fat chest-of-drawers set upon four carved and fluted legs that raised it about a foot from the ground. There were six drawers in all, two long ones in the middle and two shorter ones on either side. The serpentine front was magnificently ornamented along the top and sides and bottom, and also vertically between each set of drawers, with intricate carvings of festoons and scrolls and clusters. The brass handles, although partly obscured by white paint, appeared to be superb. It was, of course, a rather 'heavy' piece, but the design had been executed with such elegance and grace that the heaviness was in no way offensive.

'How're you feeling now?' Mr Boggis heard someone saying.

'Thank you, thank you, I'm much better already. It passes quickly. My doctor says it's nothing to worry about really so long as I rest for a few minutes whenever it happens. Ah yes,' he said, raising himself slowly to his feet. 'That's better. I'm all right now.'

A trifle unsteadily, he began to move around the room examining the furniture, one piece at a time, commenting upon it briefly. He could see at once that apart from the commode it was a very poor lot.

'Nice oak table,' he said. 'But I'm afraid it's not old enough to be of any interest. Good comfortable chairs, but quite modern, yes, quite modern. Now this cupboard, well, it's rather attractive, but again, not valuable. This chest-of-drawers' – he walked casually past the Chippendale Commode and gave it a little contemptuous flip with his fingers – 'worth a few pounds, I dare say, but no more. A rather crude reproduction, I'm afraid. Probably made in Victorian times. Did you paint it white?'

'Yes,' Rummins said, 'Bert did it.'

'A very wise move. It's considerably less offensive in white.'

'That's a strong piece of furniture,' Rummins said. 'Some nice carving on it too.'

'Machine-carved,' Mr Boggis answered superbly, bending down to examine the exquisite craftsmanship. 'You can tell it a mile off. But still, I suppose it's quite pretty in its way. It has its points.'

He began to saunter off, then he checked himself and turned

slowly back again. He placed the tip of one finger against the point of his chin, laid his head over to one side, and frowned as though deep in thought.

'You know what?' he said, looking at the commode, speaking so casually that his voice kept trailing off. 'I've just remembered . . . I've been wanting a set of legs something like that for a long time. I've got a rather curious table in my own little home, one of those low things that people put in front of the sofa, sort of a coffee-table, and last Michaelmas, when I moved house, the foolish movers damaged the legs in the most shocking way. I'm very fond of that table. I always keep my big Bible on it, and all my sermon notes.'

He paused, stroking his chin with the finger. 'Now I was just thinking. These legs on your chest-of-drawers might be very suitable. Yes, they might indeed. They could easily be cut off and fixed on to my table.'

He looked around and saw the three men standing absolutely still, watching him suspiciously, three pairs of eyes, all different but equally mistrusting, small pig-eyes for Rummins, large slow eyes for Claud, and two odd eyes for Bert, one of them very queer and boiled and misty pale, with a little black dot in the centre, like a fish eye on a plate.

Mr Boggis smiled and shook his head. 'Come, come, what on earth am I saying? I'm talking as though I owned the piece myself. I do apologize.'

'What you mean to say is you'd like to buy it,' Rummins said.

'Well . . .' Mr Boggis glanced back at the commode, frowning. 'I'm not sure. I might . . . and then again . . . on second thoughts . . . no . . . I think it might be a bit too much trouble. It's not worth it. I'd better leave it.'

 'How much were you thinking of offering?' Rummins asked.

'Not much, I'm afraid. You see, this is not a genuine antique. It's merely a reproduction.'

'I'm not so sure about that,' Rummins told him. 'It's been in *here* over twenty years, and before that it was up at the Manor House. I bought it there myself at auction when the old Squire died. You can't tell me that thing's new.'

'It's not exactly new, but it's certainly not more than about sixty years old.'

'It's more than that,' Rummins said. 'Bert, where's that bit of paper you once found at the back of one of them drawers? That old bill.'

The boy looked vacantly at his father.

Mr Boggis opened his mouth, then quickly shut it again without uttering a sound. He was beginning literally to shake with excitement, and to calm himself he walked over to the window and stared out at a plump brown hen pecking around for stray grains of corn in the yard.

'It was in the back of that drawer underneath all them rabbit-snares,' Rummins was saying. 'Go on and fetch it out and show it to the parson.'

When Bert went forward to the commode, Mr Boggis turned round again. He couldn't stand not watching him. He saw him pull out one of the big middle drawers, and he noticed the beautiful way in which the drawer slid open. He saw Bert's hand dipping inside and rummaging around among a lot of wires and strings.

'You mean this?' Bert lifted out a piece of folded yellowing paper and carried it over to the father, who unfolded it and held it up close to his face.

'You can't tell me this writing ain't bloody old,' Rummins said, and he held the paper out to Mr Boggis, whose whole arm was shaking as he took it. It was brittle and it cracked slightly between his finger. The writing was in a long sloping copperplate hand:

Edward Montagu, Esq. Dr

To Thos. Chippendale

A large mahogany Commode Table of exceeding fine wood, very rich carvd, set upon fluted legs, two very neat shapd long drawers in the middle part and two ditto on each side, with rich chasd Brass Handles and Ornaments, the whole completely finished in the most exquisite taste...£87

Mr Boggis was holding on to himself tight and fighting to suppress the excitement that was spinning round inside him and making him dizzy. Oh, God, it was wonderful! With the invoice, the value had climbed even higher. What in heaven's name would it fetch now? Twelve thousand pounds? Fourteen? Maybe fifteen or even twenty? Who knows?

Oh, boy!

He tossed the paper contemptuously on to the table and said quietly, 'It's exactly what I told you, a Victorian reproduction. This is simply the invoice that the seller – the man who made it and passed it off as an antique – gave to his client. I've seen lots of them. You'll notice that he doesn't say he made it himself. That would give the game away.'

'Say what you like,' Rummins announced, 'but that's an old piece of paper.'

'Of course it is, my dear friend. It's Victorian, late Victorian. About eighteen ninety. Sixty or seventy years old. I've seen hundreds of them. That was a time when masses of cabinet-makers did nothing else but apply themselves to faking the fine furniture of the century before.'

 'Listen, Parson,' Rummins said, pointing at him with a thick dirty finger, 'I'm not saying as how you may not know a fair bit about this furniture business, but what I *am* saying is this: How on earth can you be so mighty sure it's a fake when you haven't even seen what it looks like underneath all that paint?'

'Come here,' Mr Boggis said. 'Come over here and I'll show you.' He stood beside the commode and waited for them to gather round. 'Now, anyone got a knife?'

Claud produced a horn-handled pocket knife, and Mr Boggis took it and opened the smallest blade. Then, working with apparent casualness but actually with extreme care, he began chipping off the white paint from a small area on the top of the commode. The paint flaked away cleanly from the old hard varnish underneath, and when he had cleared away about three square inches, he stepped back and said, 'Now, take a look at that!'

It was beautiful – a warm little patch of mahogany, glowing like a topaz, rich and dark with the true colour of its two hundred years.

'What's wrong with it?' Rummins asked.

'It's processed! Anyone can see that!'

'How can you see it, Mister? You tell us.'

'Well, I must say that's a trifle difficult to explain. It's chiefly a matter of experience. My experience tells me that without the slightest doubt this wood has been processed with lime. That's what they use for mahogany, to give it that dark aged colour. For oak, they use potash salts, and for walnut it's nitric acid, but for mahogany it's always lime.'

The three men moved a little closer to peer at the wood. There was a slight stirring of interest among them now. It was always intriguing to hear about some new form of crookery or deception.

'Look closely at the grain. You see that touch of orange in among the dark red-brown. That's the sign of lime.'

They leaned forward, their noses close to the wood, first Rummins, then Claud, then Bert.

'And then there's the patina,' Mr Boggis continued.

'The what?'

He explained to them the meaning of this word as applied to furniture.

'My dear friends, you've no idea the trouble these rascals will go to to imitate the hard beautiful bronze-like appearance of genuine patina. It's terrible, really terrible, and it makes me quite sick to speak of it!' He was spitting each word sharply off the tip of the tongue and making a sour mouth to show his extreme distaste. The men waited, hoping for more secrets.

'The time and trouble that some mortals will go to in order to deceive the innocent!' Mr Boggis cried. 'It's perfectly disgusting! D'you know what they did here, my friends? I can recognize it clearly. I can almost *see* them doing it, the long, complicated ritual of rubbing the wood with linseed oil, coating it over with french polish that has been cunningly coloured, brushing it down with pumice-stone and oil, beeswaxing it with a wax that contains dirt and dust, and finally giving it the heat treatment to crack the polish so that it looks like two-hundred-year-old varnish! It really upsets me to contemplate such knavery!'

The three men continued to gaze at the little patch of dark wood.

'Feel it!' Mr Boggis ordered. 'Put your fingers on it! There, how does it feel, warm or cold?'

'Feels cold,' Rummins said.

 'Exactly, my friend! It happens to be a fact that faked patina is always cold to the touch. Real patina has a curiously warm feel to it.'

'This feels normal,' Rummins said, ready to argue.

'No, sir, it's cold. But of course it takes an experienced and sensitive finger-tip to pass a positive judgement. You couldn't really be expected to judge this any more than I could be expected to judge the quality of your barley. Everything in life, my dear sir, is experience.'

The men were staring at this queer moon-faced clergyman with the bulging eyes, not quite so suspiciously now because he did seem to know a bit about his subject. But they were still a long way from trusting him.

Mr Boggis bent down and pointed to one of the metal drawer handles on the commode. 'This is another place where the fakers go to work,' he said. 'Old brass normally has a colour and character all of its own. Did you know that?'

They stared at him, hoping for still more secrets.

'But the trouble is that they've become exceedingly skilled at matching it. In fact it's almost impossible to tell the difference between "genuine old" and "faked old". I don't mind admitting that it has me guessing. So there's not really any point in our scraping the paint off these handles. We wouldn't be any the wiser.'

'How can you possibly make new brass look like old?' Claud said. 'Brass doesn't rust, you know.'

'You are quite right, my friend. But these scoundrels have their own secret methods.'

'Such as what?' Claud asked. Any information of this nature was valuable, in his opinion. One never knew when it might come in handy.

'All they have to do,' Mr Boggis said, 'is to place these

handles overnight in a box of mahogany shavings saturated in sal ammoniac. The sal ammoniac turns the metal green, but if you rub off the green, you will find underneath it a fine soft silvery-warm lustre, a lustre identical to that which comes with very old brass. Oh, it is so bestial, the things they do! With iron they have another trick.'

'What do they do with iron?' Claud asked, fascinated.

'Iron's easy,' Mr Boggis said. 'Iron locks and plates and hinges are simply buried in common salt and they come out all rusted and pitted in no time.'

'All right,' Rummins said. 'So you admit you can't tell about the handles. For all you know, they may be hundreds and hundreds of years old. Correct?'

'Ah,' Mr Boggis whispered, fixing Rummins with two big bulging brown eyes. 'That's where you're wrong. Watch this.'

From his jacket pocket, he took out a small screwdriver. At the same time, although none of them saw him do it, he also took out a little brass screw which he kept well hidden in the palm of his hand. Then he selected one of the screws in the commode – there were four to each handle – and began carefully scraping all traces of white paint from its head. When he had done this, he started slowly to unscrew it.

'If this is a genuine old brass screw from the eighteenth century,' he was saying, 'the spiral will be slightly uneven and you'll be able to see quite easily that it has been hand-cut with a file. But if this brasswork is faked from more recent times, Victorian or later, then obviously the screw will be of the same period. It will be a mass-produced, machine made article. Anyone can recognize a machine-made screw. Well, we shall see.'

It was not difficult, as he put his hands over the old screw and drew it out, for Mr Boggis to substitute the new one hidden in his palm. This was another little trick of his, and through the years it had proved a most rewarding one. The pockets of his clergyman's jacket were always stocked with a quantity of cheap brass screws of various sizes.

'There you are,' he said, handing the modern screw to Rummins. 'Take a look at that. Notice the exact evenness of the spiral? See it? Of course you do. It's just a cheap common little screw you yourself could buy today in any ironmonger's in the country.'

The screw was handed round from the one to the other, each examining it carefully. Even Rummins was impressed now.

Mr Boggis put the screwdriver back in his pocket together with the fine hand-cut screw that he'd taken from the commode, and then he turned and walked slowly past the three men towards the door.

'My dear friends,' he said, pausing at the entrance to the kitchen, 'it was so good of you to let me peep inside your little home – so kind. I do hope I haven't been a terrible old bore.'

Rummins glanced up from examining the screw. 'You didn't tell us what you were going to offer,' he said.

'Ah,' Mr Boggis said. 'That's quite right. I didn't, did I? Well, to tell you the honest truth, I think it's all a bit too much trouble. I think I'll leave it.'

'How much would you give?'

'You mean that you really wish to part with it?'

'I didn't say I wished to part with it. I asked you how much.'

Mr Boggis looked across at the commode, and he laid his head first to one side, then to the other, and he frowned, and pushed out his lips, and shrugged his shoulders, and gave a little scornful wave of the hand as though to say the thing was hardly worth thinking about really, was it?

'Shall we say . . . ten pounds. I think that would be fair.'

'Ten pounds!' Rummins cried. 'Don't be so ridiculous, Parson, *please*!'

'It's worth more'n that for firewood!' Claud said, disgusted.

'Look here at the bill!' Rummins went on, stabbing that precious document so fiercely with his dirty fore-finger that Mr Boggis became alarmed. 'It tells you exactly what it cost! Eighty-seven pounds! And that's when it was new. Now it's antique it's worth double!'

'If you'll pardon me, no, sir, it's not. It's a second-hand reproduction. But I'll tell you what, my friend – I'm being rather reckless, I can't help it – I'll go up as high as fifteen pounds. How's that?'

'Make it fifty,' Rummins said.

A delicious little quiver like needles ran all the way down the back of Mr Boggis's legs and then under the soles of his feet. He had it now. It was his. No question about that. But the habit of buying cheap, as cheap as it was humanly possible to buy, acquired by years of necessity and practice, was too strong in him now to permit him to give in so easily.

'My dear man,' he whispered softly, 'I only *want* the legs. Possibly I could find some use for the drawers later on, but the rest of it, the carcass itself, as your friend so rightly said, it's firewood, that's all.'

'Make it thirty-five,' Rummins said.

'I *couldn't* sir, I *couldn't*! It's not worth it. And I simply mustn't allow myself to haggle like this about a price. It's all wrong. I'll make you one final offer, and then I must go. Twenty pounds.'

'I'll take it,' Rummins snapped. 'It's yours.'

'Oh dear,' Mr Boggis said, clasping his hands. 'There I go again. I should never have started this in the first place.'

'You can't back out now, Parson. A deal's a deal.'

'Yes, yes, I know.'

'How're you going to take it?'

'Well, let me see. Perhaps if I were to drive my car up into the yard, you gentlemen would be kind enough to help me load it?'

'In a car? This thing'll never go in a car! You'll need a truck for this!'

'I don't think so. Anyway, we'll see. My car's on the road. I'll be back in a jiffy. We'll manage it somehow, I'm sure.'

Mr Boggis walked out into the yard and through the gate and then down the long track that led across the field towards the road. He found himself giggling quite uncontrollably, and there was a feeling inside him as though hundreds and hundreds of tiny bubbles were rising up from his stomach and bursting merrily in the top of his head, like sparkling-water. All the buttercups in the field were suddenly turning into golden sovereigns, glistening in the sunlight. The ground was littered with them, and he swung off the track on to the grass so that he could walk among them and tread on them and hear the little metallic tinkle they made as he kicked them around with his toes. He was finding it difficult to stop himself from breaking into a run. But clergymen never run they walk slowly. Walk slowly, Boggis. Keep calm, Boggis. There's no hurry now. The commode is yours! Yours for twenty pounds, and it's worth fifteen or twenty thousand! The Boggis Commode! In ten minutes it'll be loaded into your car – it'll go in easily – and you'll be driving back to London and singing all the way! Mr Boggis driving the Boggis Commode home in the Boggis car. Historic occasion. What *wouldn't* a newspaperman give to get a picture of that! Should he arrange it? Perhaps he should. Wait and see. Oh, glorious day! Oh, lovely sunny summer day! Oh, glory be!

Back in the farmhouse, Rummins was saying, 'Fancy that old bastard giving twenty pound for a load of junk like this.'

'You did very nicely, Mr Rummins,' Claud told him. 'You think he'll pay you?'

'We don't put it in the car till he do.'

'And what if it won't go in the car?' Claud asked. 'You know what I think, Mr Rummins? You want my honest opinion? I think the bloody thing's too big to go in the car. And then what happens? Then he's going to say to hell with it and just drive off without it and you'll never see him again. Nor the money either. He didn't seem all that keen on having it, you know.'

Rummins paused to consider this new and rather alarming prospect.

'How can a thing like that possibly go in a car?' Claud went on relentlessly. 'A parson never has a big car anyway. You ever seen a parson with a big car, Mr Rummins?'

'Can't say I have.'

'Exactly! And now listen to me. I've got an idea. He told us, didn't he, that it was only the legs he was wanting. Right? So all we've got to do is to cut 'em off quick right here on the spot before he comes back, then it'll be sure to go in the car. All we're doing is saving him the trouble of cutting them off himself when he gets home. How about it, Mr Rummins?' Claud's flat bovine face glimmered with a mawkish pride.

'It's not such a bad idea at that,' Rummins said, looking at the commode. 'In fact it's a bloody good idea. Come on then, we'll have to hurry. You and Bert carry it out into the yard. I'll get the saw. Take the drawers out first.'

Within a couple of minutes, Claud and Bert had carried the commode outside and had laid it upside down in the yard amidst the chicken droppings and cow dung and mud. In the distance, half-way across the field, they could see a small black figure striding along the path towards the road. They paused to watch. There was something rather comical about the way in which this figure was conducting itself. Every now and again it would break into a trot, then it did a kind of hop, skip, and jump, and once it seemed as though the sound of a cheerful song came rippling faintly to them from across the meadow.

'I reckon he's barmy,' Claud said, and Bert grinned darkly, rolling his misty eye slowly round in its socket.

Rummins came waddling over from the shed, squat and froglike, carrying a long saw. Claud took the saw away from him and went to work.

'Cut 'em close,' Rummins said. 'Don't forget he's going to use 'em on another table.'

The mahogany was hard and very dry, and as Claud worked, a fine red dust sprayed out from the edge of the saw and fell softly to the ground. One by one, the legs came off, and when they were all severed, Bert stooped down and arranged them carefully in a row.

Claud stepped back to survey the results of his labour. There was a longish pause.

'Just let me ask you one question, Mr Rummins,' he said slowly. 'Even now, could *you* put that enormous thing into the back of a car?'

'Not unless it was a van.'

'Correct!' Claud cried. 'And parsons don't have vans, you know. All they've got usually is piddling little Morris Eights or Austin Sevens.'

'The legs is all he wants,' Rummins said. 'If the rest of it won't go in, then he can leave it. He can't complain. He's got the legs.'

'Now you know better'n that, Mr Rummins,' Claud said patiently. 'You know damn well he's going to start knocking the price if he don't get every single bit of this into the car. A parson's just as cunning as the rest of 'em when it comes to money, don't you make any mistake about that. Especially this old boy. So why don't we give him his firewood now and be done with it. Where d'you keep the axe?'

'I reckon that's fair enough,' Rummins said. 'Bert, go fetch the axe.'

Bert went into the shed and fetched a tall woodcutter's axe and gave it to Claud. Claud spat on the palms of his hands and rubbed them together. Then, with a long-armed high-swinging action, he began fiercely attacking the legless carcass of the commode.

It was hard work, and it took several minutes before he had the whole thing more or less smashed to pieces.

'I'll tell you one thing,' he said, straightening up, wiping his brow. 'That was a bloody good carpenter put this job together and I don't care what the parson says.'

'We're just in time!' Rummins called out. 'Here he comes!'

A Piece of Cake

I do not remember much of it; not beforehand anyway; not until it happened.

There was the landing at Fouka, where the Blenheim boys were helpful and gave us tea while we were being refuelled. I remember the quietness of the Blenheim boys, how they came into the mess-tent to get some tea and sat down to drink it without saying anything; how they got up and went out when they had finished drinking and still they did not say anything. And I knew that each one was holding himself together because the going was not very good right then. They were having to go out too often, and there were no replacements coming along.

We thanked them for the tea and went out to see if they had finished refuelling our Gladiators. I remember that there was a wind blowing which made the windsock stand out straight, like a signpost, and the sand was blowing up around our legs and making a rustling noise as it swished against the tents, and the tents flapped in the wind so that they were like canvas men clapping their hands.

'Bomber boys unhappy,' Peter said.

'Not unhappy,' I answered.

'Well, they're browned off.'

'No. They've had it, that's all. But they'll keep going. You can see they're trying to keep going.'

Our two old Gladiators were standing beside each other in the sand and the airmen in their khaki shirts and shorts seemed still to be busy with the refuelling. I was wearing a thin white cotton flying suit and Peter had on a blue one. It wasn't necessary to fly with anything warmer.

Peter said, 'How far away is it?'

'Twenty-one miles beyond Charing Cross,' I answered, 'on the right side of the road.' Charing Cross was where the desert road branched north to Mersah Matruh. The Italian army was outside Mersah, and they were doing pretty well. It was about the only time, so far as I know, that the Italians have done pretty well. Their morale goes up and down like a sensitive altimeter, and right then it was at forty thousand because the Axis was on top of the world. We hung around waiting for the refuelling to finish.

Peter said, 'It's a piece of cake.'

'Yes. It ought to be easy.'

We separated and I climbed into my cockpit. I have always remembered the face of the airman who helped me to strap in. He was oldish, about forty, and bald except for a neat patch of golden hair at the back of his head. His face was all wrinkles, his eyes were like my grandmother's eyes, and he looked as though he had spent his life helping to strap in pilots who never came back. He stood on the wing pulling my straps and said, 'Be careful. There isn't any sense not being careful.'

'Piece of cake,' I said.

'Like hell.'

'Really. It isn't anything at all. It's a piece of cake.'

I don't remember much about the next bit; I only remember about later on. I suppose we took off from Fouka and flew west towards Mersah, and I suppose we flew at about eight hundred feet. I suppose we saw the sea to starboard and I suppose – no, I am certain – that it was blue and that it was beautiful, especially

 where it rolled up on to the sand and made a long thick white line east and west as far as you could see. I suppose we flew over Charing Cross and flew on for twenty-one miles to where they had said it would be, but I do not know. I know only that there was trouble, lots and lots of trouble, and I know that we had turned round and were coming back when the trouble got worse. The biggest trouble of all was that I was too low to bale out, and it is from that point on that my memory comes back to me. I remember the dipping of the nose of the aircraft and I remember looking down the nose of the machine at the ground and seeing a little clump of camel-thorn growing there all by itself, I remember seeing some rocks lying in the sand beside the camel-thorn, and the camel-thorn and the sand and the rocks leapt out of the ground and came to me. I remember that very clearly.

Then there was a small gap of not-remembering. It might have been one second or it might have been thirty; I do not know. I have an idea that it was very short, a second perhaps, and next I heard a *crumph* on the right as the starboard wing tank caught fire, then another *crumph* on the left as the port tank did the same. To me that was not significant, and for a while I sat still, feeling comfortable, but a little drowsy. I couldn't see with my eyes, but that was not significant either. There was nothing to worry about. Nothing at all. Not until I felt the hotness around my legs. At first it was only a warmness and that was all right too, but all at once it was a hotness, a very stinging scorching hotness up and down the sides of each leg.

I knew that the hotness was unpleasant, but that was all I knew. I disliked it, so I curled my legs up under the seat and waited. I think there was something wrong with the telegraph system between the body and the brain. It did not seem to be working very well. Somehow it was a bit slow in telling the brain all about it and in asking for instructions. But I believe a message eventually got through, saying, 'Down here there is a great hotness. What shall we do? (Signed) Left Leg and Right Leg.' For a long time there was no reply. The brain was figuring the matter out.

Then slowly, word by word, the answer was tapped over the wires. 'The – plane – is – burning. Get – out – repeat – get – out – get – out.' The order was relayed to the whole system, to all the muscles in the legs, arms and body, and the muscles went to work. They tried their best; they pushed a little and pulled a little, and they strained greatly, but it wasn't any good. Up went another telegram, 'Can't get out. Something holding us in.' The answer to this one took even longer in arriving, so I just sat there waiting for it to come, and all the time the hotness increased. Something was holding me down and it was up to the brain to find out what it was. Was it giants' hands pressing on my shoulders, or heavy stones or houses or steam rollers or filing cabinets or gravity or was it ropes? Wait a minute. Ropes – ropes. The message was beginning to come through. It came very slowly. 'Your – straps. Undo – your – straps.' My arms received the message and went to work. They tugged at the straps, but they wouldn't undo. They tugged again and again, a little feebly, but as hard as they could, and it wasn't any use. Back went the message. 'How do we undo the straps?'

This time I think that I sat there for three or four minutes waiting for the answer. It wasn't any use hurrying or getting impatient. That was the one thing of which I was sure. But what a long time it was all taking. I said aloud, 'Bugger it. I'm going to be burnt. I'm . . .' but I was interrupted. The answer was coming – no, it wasn't – yes, it was, it was slowly coming through. 'Pull – out – the – quick – release – pin – you – bloody – fool – and – hurry.'

Out came the pin and the straps were loosed. Now, let's get out. Let's get out, let's get out. But I couldn't do it. I simply couldn't lift myself out of the cockpit. Arms and legs tried their best but it wasn't any use. A last desperate message was flashed upwards and this time it was marked 'Urgent.'

'Something else is holding us down,' it said. 'Something else, something else, something heavy.'

Still the arms and legs did not fight. They seemed to know instinctively that there was no point in using up their strength. They stayed quiet and waited for the answer, and oh what a time it took. Twenty, thirty, forty hot seconds. None of them really white hot yet, no sizzling of flesh or smell of burning meat, but that would come any moment now, because those old Gladiators aren't made of stressed steel like a Hurricane or a Spit. They have taut canvas wings, covered with magnificently inflammable dope, and underneath there are hundreds of small thin sticks, the kind you put under the logs for kindling, only these are drier and thinner. If a clever man said, 'I am going to build a big thing that will burn better and quicker than anything else in the world,' and if he applied himself diligently to his task he would probably finish up by building something very like a Gladiator. I sat still waiting.

Then suddenly the reply, beautiful in its briefness, but at the same time explaining everything. 'Your – parachute – turn – the – buckle.'

I turned the buckle, released the parachute harness and with some effort hoisted myself up and tumbled over the side of the cockpit. Something seemed to be burning, so I rolled about a bit in the sand, then crawled away from the fire on all fours and lay down.

I heard some of my machine-gun ammunition going off in the

heat and I heard some of the bullets thumping into the sand near by. I did not worry about them; I merely heard them.

Things were beginning to hurt. My face hurt most. There was something wrong with my face. Something had happened to it. Slowly I put up a hand to feel it. It was sticky. My nose didn't seem to be there. I tried to feel my teeth but I cannot remember whether I came to any conclusion about them. I think I dozed off.

All of a sudden there was Peter. I heard his voice and I heard him dancing around and yelling like a madman and shaking my hand and saying, 'Jesus, I thought you were still inside. I came down half a mile away and ran like hell. Are you all right?'

I said, 'Peter, what has happened to my nose?'

I heard him striking a match in the dark. The night comes quickly in the desert. There was a pause.

'It actually doesn't seem to be there very much,' he said. 'Does it hurt?'

'Don't be a bloody fool, of course it hurts.'

He said he was going back to his machine to get some morphia out of his emergency pack, but he came back again soon, saying he couldn't find his aircraft in the dark.

'Peter,' I said, 'I can't see anything.'

'It's night,' he answered. 'I can't see either.'

It was cold now. It was bitter cold, and Peter lay down close alongside so that we could both keep a little warmer. Every now and then he would say, 'I've never seen a man without a nose before,' I kept spewing a lot of blood and every time I did it, Peter lit a match. Once he gave me a cigarette, but it got wet and I didn't want it anyway.

I do not know how long we stayed there and I remember only very little more. I remember that I kept telling Peter that there was a tin of sore throat tablets, in my pocket, and that he should take one, otherwise he would catch my sore throat. I remember asking him where we were and him saying, 'We're between the two armies,' and then I remember English voices from an English patrol asking if we were Italians. Peter said something to them; I cannot remember what he said.

Later I remember hot thick soup and one spoonful making me sick. And all the time the pleasant feeling that Peter was around, being wonderful, doing wonderful things and never going away. That is all that I can remember.

The men stood beside the airplane painting away and talking about the heat.

'Painting pictures on the aircraft,' I said.

'Yes,' said Peter. 'It's a great idea. It's subtle.'

'Why?' I said. 'Just you tell me.'

'They're funny pictures,' he said. 'The German pilots will all laugh when they see them; they'll shake so with their laughing that they won't be able to shoot straight.'

'Oh baloney baloney baloney.'

'No, it's a great idea. It's fine. Come and have a look.'

We ran towards the line of aircraft. 'Hop, skip, jump,' said Peter. 'Hop skip jump, keep in time.'

'Hop skip jump,' I said, 'Hop skip jump,' and we danced along.

The painter on the first aeroplane had a straw hat on his head and a sad face. He was copying the drawing out of a magazine, and when Peter saw it he said, 'Boy oh boy look at that picture,' and he began to laugh. His laugh began with a rumble and grew quickly into a belly-roar and he slapped his thighs with his hands both at the same time and went on laughing with his body doubled up and his mouth wide open and his eyes shut. His silk top hat fell off his head on to the sand.

'That's not funny,' I said.

'Not funny!' he cried. 'What d'you mean "not funny"? Look at me. Look at me laughing. Laughing like this I couldn't hit anything. I couldn't hit a hay wagon or a house or a louse.' And he capered about on the sand, gurgling and shaking with laughter. Then he seized me by the arm and we danced over to the next aeroplane. 'Hop skip jump,' he said. 'Hop skip jump.'

There was a small man with a crumpled face writing a long story on the fuselage with a red crayon. His straw hat was perched straight on the back of his head and his face was shiny with sweat.

'Good morning,' he said. 'Good morning, good morning,' and he swept his hat off his head in a very elegant way.

Peter said, 'Shut up,' and bent down and began to read what the little man had been writing. All the time Peter was spluttering and rumbling with laughter, and as he read he began to laugh afresh. He rocked from one side to the other and danced around on the sand slapping his thighs with his hands and bending his body. 'Oh my, what a story, what a story, what a story. Look at me. Look at me laughing,' and he hopped about on his toes, shaking his head and chortling like a madman. Then suddenly I saw the joke and I began to laugh with him. I laughed so much that my stomach hurt and I fell down and rolled around on the sand and roared and roared because it was so funny that there was nothing else I could do.

'Peter, you're marvellous,' I shouted. 'But can all those German pilots read English?'

'Oh hell,' he said. 'Oh hell. Stop,' he shouted. 'Stop your work,' and the painters all stopped their painting and turned round slowly and looked at Peter. They did a little caper on their toes and began to chant in unison. 'Rubbishy things – on all the wings, on all the wings, on all the wings,' they chanted.

'Shut up,' said Peter. 'We're in a jam. We must keep calm. Where's my top hat?'

'What?' I said.

'You can speak German,' he said. 'You must translate for us. He will translate for you,' he shouted to the painters. 'He will translate.'

Then I saw his black top hat lying in the sand. I looked away, then I looked around and saw it again. It was a silk opera hat and it was lying there on its side in the sand.

'You're mad,' I shouted. 'You're madder than hell. You don't know what you're doing. You'll get us all killed. You're absolutely plumb crazy, do you know that? You're crazier than hell. My God, you're crazy.'

'Goodness, what a noise you're making. You mustn't shout like that: it's not good for you.' This was a woman's voice. 'You've made yourself all hot,' she said, and I felt someone wiping my forehead with a handkerchief. 'You mustn't work yourself up like that.'

Then she was gone and I saw only the sky, which was pale blue. There were no clouds and all around were the German fighters. They were above, below and on every side and there was no way I could go; there was nothing I could do. They took it in turns to come in to attack and they flew their aircraft carelessly, banking and looping and dancing in the air. But I was not frightened, because of the funny pictures on my wings. I was confident and I thought, 'I am going to fight a hundred of them alone and I'll shoot them all down. I'll shoot them while they are laughing; that's what I'll do.'

Then they flew closer. The whole sky was full of them. There were so many that I did not know which ones to watch and which ones to attack. There were so many that they made a black curtain over the sky and only here and there could I see a little of the blue showing through. But there was enough to patch a Dutchman's trousers, which was all that mattered. So long as there was enough to do that, then everything was all right.

Still they flew closer. They came nearer and nearer, right up in front of my face so that I saw only the black crosses which stood out brightly against the colour of the Messerschmitts and against the blue of the sky; and as I turned my head quickly from one side to the other I saw more aircraft and more crosses and then I saw nothing but the arms of the crosses and the blue of the sky. The arms had hands and they joined together and made a circle and danced around my Gladiator, while the engines of the Messerschmitts sang joyfully in a deep voice. They were playing Oranges and Lemons and every now and then two would detach themselves and come out into the middle of the floor and make an attack and I knew then that it was Oranges and Lemons. They banked and swerved and danced upon their toes and they leant against the air first to one side, then to the other. 'Oranges and Lemons said the bells of St Clements,' sang the engines.

But I was still confident. I could dance better than they and I had a better partner. She was the most beautiful girl in the world. I looked down and saw the curve of her neck and the gentle slope of her pale shoulders and I saw her slender arms eager and outstretched.

Suddenly I saw some bullet holes in my starboard wing and I got angry and scared both at the same time; but mostly I got angry. Then I got confident and I said, 'The German who did that had no sense of humour. There's always one man in a party who has no sense of humour. But there's nothing to worry about; there's nothing at all to worry about.'

Then I saw more bullet holes and I got scared. I slid back the hood of the cockpit and stood up and shouted, 'You fools, look at the funny pictures. Look at the one on my tail; look at the story on my fuselage. Please look at the story on my fuselage.'

But they kept on coming. They tripped into the middle of the floor in twos, shooting at me as they came. And the engines of the Messerschmitts sang loudly. 'When will you pay me, said the bells of Old Bailey?' sang the engines, and as they sang the black crosses danced and swayed to the rhythm of the music. There were more holes in my wings, in the engine cowling and in the cockpit.

Then suddenly there were some in my body.

But there was no pain, even when I went into a spin, when the wings of my plane went flip, flip, flip flip, faster and faster, when the blue sky and the black sea chased each other round and round until there was no longer any sky or sea but just the flashing of the sun as I turned. But the black crosses were following me down, still dancing and still holding hands and I could still hear the singing of their engines. 'Here comes a candle to light you to bed, here comes a chopper to chop off your head,' sang the engines.

Still the wings went flip, flip, flip flip, and there was neither sky nor sea around me, but only the sun.

Then there was only the sea. I could see it below me and I could see the white horses, and I said to myself, 'Those are white horses riding a rough sea.' I knew then that my brain was going well because of the white horses and because of the sea. I knew that there was not much time because the sea and the white horses were nearer, the white horses were bigger and the sea was like a sea and like water, not like a smooth plate. Then there was only one white horse, rushing forward madly with his bit in his teeth, foaming at the mouth, scattering the spray with his hooves and arching his neck as he ran. He galloped on madly over the sea, riderless and uncontrollable, and I could tell that we were going to crash.

After that it was warmer, and there were no black crosses and there was no sky. But it was only warm because it was not hot and it was not cold. I was sitting in a great red chair made of velvet and it was evening. There was a wind blowing from behind.

'Where am I?' I said.

'You are missing. You are missing, believed killed.'

'Then I must tell my mother.'

'You can't. You can't use that phone.'

'Why not?'

'It goes only to God.'

'What did you say I was?'

'Missing, believed killed.'

'That's not true. It's a lie. It's a lousy lie because here I am and I'm not missing. You're just trying to frighten me and you won't succeed. You won't succeed, I tell you, because I know it's a lie and I'm going back to my squadron. You can't stop me because I'll just go. I'm going, you see. I'm going.'

I got up from the red chair and began to run.

'Let me see those X-rays again, nurse.'

'They're here, doctor.' This was the woman's voice again, and now it came closer. 'You have been making a noise tonight, haven't you? Let me straighten your pillow for you, you're pushing it on to the floor.' The voice was close and it was very soft and nice.

'Am I missing?'

'No, of course not. You're fine.'

'They said I was missing.'

'Don't be silly; you're fine.'

Oh everyone's silly, silly, silly, but it was a lovely day, and I did not want to run but I couldn't stop because my legs were carrying me and I had no control over them. It was as if they did not belong to me, although when I looked down I saw that they were mine, that the shoes on the feet were mine and that the legs were joined to my body. But they would not do what I wanted; they just went on running across the field and I had to go with them. I ran and ran and ran, and although in some places the field was rough and bumpy, I never stumbled. I ran past trees and hedges and in one field there were some sheep which stopped their eating and scampered off as I ran past them. Once I saw my mother in a pale grey dress bending down picking mushrooms, and as I ran past she looked up and said, 'My basket's nearly full; shall we go home soon?' but my legs wouldn't stop and I had to go on.

Then I saw the cliff ahead and I saw how dark it was beyond the cliff. There was the great cliff and beyond it there was nothing but darkness, although the sun was shining in the field where I was running. The light of the sun stopped dead at the edge of the cliff and there was only darkness beyond. 'That must be where the night begins,' I thought, and once more I tried to stop but it was not any good. My legs began to go faster towards the cliff and they began to take longer strides, and I reached down with my hand and tried to stop them by clutching the cloth of my trousers, but it did not work; then I tried to fall down. But my legs were nimble, and each time I threw myself I landed on my toes and went on running.

Now the cliff and the darkness were much nearer and I could see that unless I stopped quickly I should go over the edge. Once more I tried to throw myself to the ground and once more I landed on my toes and went on running.

I was going fast as I came to the edge and I went straight on over it into the darkness and began to fall.

At first it was not quite dark. I could see little trees growing out of the face of the cliff, and I grabbed at them with my hands as I went down. Several times I managed to catch hold of a branch, but it always broke off at once because I was so heavy and because I was falling so fast, and once I caught a thick branch with both hands and the tree leaned forward and I heard the snapping of the roots one by one until it came away from the cliff and I went on falling. Then it became darker because the sun and the day were in the fields far away at the top of the cliff, and as I fell I kept my eyes open and watched the darkness turn from grey-black to black, from black to jet black and from jet black to pure liquid blackness which I could touch with my hands but which I could not see. But I went on falling, and it was so black that there was nothing anywhere and it was not any use doing anything or caring or thinking because of the blackness and because of the falling. It was not any use.

'You're better this morning. You're much better.' It was the woman's voice again.

'Hallo.'

'Hallo; we thought you were never going to get conscious.'

'Where am I?'

'In Alexandria; in hospital.'

'How long have I been here?'

'Four days.'

'What time is it?'

'Seven o'clock in the morning.'

'Why can't I see?'

I heard her walking a little closer.

'Oh, we've just put a bandage around your eyes for a bit.'

'How long for?'

'Just for a while. Don't worry. You're fine. You were very lucky, you know.'

I was feeling my face with my fingers but I couldn't feel it; I could only feel something else.

'What's wrong with my face?'

I heard her coming up to the side of my bed and I felt her hand touching my shoulder.

'You mustn't talk any more. You're not allowed to talk. It's bad for you. Just lie still and don't worry. You're fine.'

I heard the sound of her footsteps as she walked across the floor and I heard her open the door and shut it again.

'Nurse,' I said. 'Nurse.'

But she was gone.

Lamb to the Slaughter

The room was warm and clean, the curtains drawn, the two table lamps alight – hers and the one by the empty chair opposite. On the sideboard behind her, two tall glasses, soda water, whisky. Fresh ice cubes in the Thermos bucket.

Mary Maloney was waiting for her husband to come home from work.

Now and again she would glance up at the clock but without anxiety, merely to please herself with the thought that each minute gone by made it nearer the time when he would come. There was a slow smiling air about her, and about everything she did. The drop of the head as she bent over her sewing was curiously tranquil. Her skin – for this was her sixth month with child – had acquired a wonderful translucent quality, the mouth was soft, and the eyes, with their new placid look seemed larger, darker than before.

When the clock said ten minutes to five, she began to listen, and a few moments later, punctually as always, she heard the tyres on the gravel outside, and the car door slamming, the footsteps passing the window, the key turning in the lock. She laid aside her sewing, stood up, and went forward to kiss him as he came in.

'Hallo, darling,' she said.

'Hallo,' he answered.

She took his coat and hung it in the closet. Then she walked over and made the drinks, a strongish one for him, a weak one for herself and soon she was back again in her chair with the sewing, and he in the other, opposite, holding the tall glass with both his hands, rocking it so the ice cubes tinkled against the side.

For her, this was always a blissful time of day. She knew he didn't want to speak much until the first drink was finished, and she, on her side, was content to sit quietly, enjoying his company after the long hours alone in the house. She loved to luxuriate in the presence of this man, and to feel – almost as a sunbather feels the sun – that warm male glow that came out of him to her when they were alone together. She loved him for the way he sat loosely in a chair, for the way he came in a door, or moved slowly across the room with long strides. She loved the intent, far look in his eyes when they rested on her, the funny shape of the mouth, and especially the way he remained silent about his tiredness, sitting still with himself until the whisky had taken some of it away.

'Tired, darling?'

'Yes,' he said. 'I'm tired.' And as he spoke, he did an unusual thing. He lifted his glass and drained it in one swallow although there was still half of it, at least half of it, left. She wasn't really watching him but she knew what he had done because she heard the ice cubes falling back against the bottom of the empty glass when he lowered his arm. He paused a moment, leaning forward in the chair, then he got up and went slowly over to fetch himself another.

'I'll get it!' she cried, jumping up.

'Sit down,' he said.

When he came back, she noticed that the new drink was dark amber with the quantity of whisky in it.

'Darling, shall I get your slippers?'

'No.'

She watched him as he began to sip the dark yellow drink, and she could see little oily swirls in the liquid because it was so strong.

'I think it's a shame,' she said, 'that when a policeman gets to be as senior as you, they keep him walking about on his feet all day long.'

He didn't answer, so she bent her head again and went on with her sewing; but each time he lifted the drink to his lips, she heard the ice cubes clinking against the side of the glass.

'Darling,' she said. 'Would you like me to get you some cheese? I haven't made any supper because it's Thursday.'

'No,' he said.

'If you're too tired to eat out,' she went on, 'it's still not too late. There's plenty of meat and stuff in the freezer, and you can have it right here and not even move out of the chair.'

Her eyes waited on him for an answer, a smile, a little nod, but he made no sign.

'Anyway,' she went on, 'I'll get you some cheese and crackers first.'

'I don't want it,' he said.

She moved uneasily in her chair, the large eyes still watching his face. 'But you *must* have supper. I can easily do it here. I'd like to do it. We can have lamb chops. Or pork. Anything you want. Everything's in the freezer.'

'Forget it,' he said.

'But, darling, you *must* eat! I'll fix it anyway, and then you can have it or not, as you like.'

She stood up and placed her sewing on the table by the lamp.

'Sit down,' he said. 'Just for a minute, sit down.'

It wasn't till then that she began to get frightened.

'Go on,' he said. 'Sit down.'

She lowered herself back slowly into the chair, watching him all the time with those large, bewildered eyes. He had finished the second drink and was staring down into the glass frowning.

'Listen,' he said, 'I've got something to tell you.'

'What is it, darling? What's the matter?'

He had become absolutely motionless, and he kept his head down so that the light from the lamp beside him fell across the upper part of his face, leaving the chin and mouth in shadow. She noticed there was a little muscle moving near the corner of his left eye.

'This is going to be a bit of a shock to you, I'm afraid,' he said. 'But I've thought about it a good deal and I've decided the only thing to do is tell you right away. I hope you won't blame me too much.'

And he told her. It didn't take long, four or five minutes at most, and she sat very still through it all, watching him with a kind of dazed horror as he went further and further away from her with each word.

'So there it is,' he added. 'And I know it's kind of a bad time to be telling you, but there simply wasn't any other way. Of course I'll give you money and see you're looked after. But there needn't really be any fuss. I hope not anyway. It wouldn't be very good for my job.'

Her first instinct was not to believe any of it, to reject it all. It occurred to her that perhaps he hadn't even spoken, that she herself had imagined the whole thing. Maybe, if she went about her business and acted as though she hadn't been listening, then later, when she sort of woke up again, she might find none of it had ever happened.

'I'll get the supper,' she managed to whisper, and this time he didn't stop her.

When she walked across the room she couldn't feel her feet touching the floor. She couldn't feel anything at all – except a slight nausea and a desire to vomit. Everything was automatic now – down the stairs to the cellar, the light switch, the deep freeze, the hand inside the cabinet taking hold of the first object it met. She lifted it out, and looked at it. It was wrapped in paper, so she took off the paper and looked at it again.

A leg of lamb.

All right then, they would have lamb for supper. She carried it upstairs, holding the thin bone-end of it with both her hands, and as she went through the living-room, she saw him standing over by the window with his back to her, and she stopped.

'For God's sake,' he said, hearing her, but not turning round. 'Don't make supper for me. I'm going out.'

At that point, Mary Maloney simply walked up behind him and without any pause she swung the big frozen leg of lamb high in the air and brought it down as hard as she could on the back of his head.

She might just as well have hit him with a steel club.

She stepped back a pace, waiting, and the funny thing was that he remained standing there for at least four or five seconds, gently swaying. Then he crashed to the carpet.

The violence of the crash, the noise, the small table overturning, helped bring her out of the shock. She came out slowly, feeling cold and surprised, and she stood for a while blinking at the body, still holding the ridiculous piece of meat tight with both hands.

All right, she told herself. So I've killed him.

It was extraordinary, now, how clear her mind became all of a sudden. She began thinking very fast. As the wife of a detective, she knew quite well what the penalty would be. That was fine. It made no difference to her. In fact, it would be a relief. On the other hand, what about the child? What were the laws about murderers with unborn children? Did they kill them both – mother and child? Or did they wait until the tenth month? What did they do?

Mary Maloney didn't know. And she certainly wasn't prepared to take a chance.

She carried the meat into the kitchen, placed it in a pan, turned the oven on high, and shoved it inside. Then she washed her hands and ran upstairs to the bedroom. She sat down before the mirror, tidied her face, touched up her lips and face. She tried a smile. It came out rather peculiar. She tried again.

'Hallo, Sam,' she said brightly, aloud.

The voice sounded peculiar too.

'I want some potatoes please, Sam. Yes, and I think a can of peas.'

That was better. Both the smile and the voice were coming out better now. She rehearsed it several times more. Then she ran downstairs, took her coat, went out the back door, down the garden, into the street.

It wasn't six o'clock yet and the lights were still on in the grocery shop.

'Hallo, Sam,' she said brightly, smiling at the man behind the counter.

'Why, good evening, Mrs Maloney. How're *you*?'

'I want some potatoes please, Sam. Yes, and I think a can of peas.'

The man turned and reached up behind him on the shelf for the peas.

'Patrick's decided he's tired and doesn't want to eat out

tonight,' she told him. 'We usually go out Thursdays, you know, and now he's caught me without any vegetables in the house.'

'Then how about meat, Mrs Maloney?'

'No, I've got meat, thanks. I got a nice leg of lamb, from the freezer.'

'Oh.'

'I don't much like cooking it frozen, Sam, but I'm taking a chance on it this time. You think it'll be all right?'

'Personally,' the grocer said, 'I don't believe it makes any difference. You want these Idaho potatoes?'

'Oh yes, that'll be fine. Two of those.'

'Anything else?' The grocer cocked his head on one side, looking at her pleasantly. 'How about afterwards? What you going to give him for afterwards?'

'Well – what would you suggest, Sam?'

The man glanced around his shop. 'How about a nice big slice of cheesecake? I know he likes that.'

'Perfect,' she said. 'He loves it.'

And when it was all wrapped and she had paid she put on her brightest smile and said, 'Thank you, Sam. Good night.'

'Good night, Mrs Maloney. And thank *you*.'

And now, she told herself as she hurried back, all she was doing now, she was returning home to her husband and he was waiting for his supper; and she must cook it good, and make it as tasty as possible because the poor man was tired; and if, when she entered the house, she happened to find anything unusual, or tragic, or terrible, then naturally it would be a shock and she'd become frantic with grief and horror. Mind you, she wasn't *expecting* to find anything. She was just going home with the vegetables. Mrs Patrick Maloney going home with the vegetables on Thursday evening to cook supper for her husband.

That's the way, she told herself. Do everything right and natural. Keep things absolutely natural and there'll be no need for any acting at all.

Therefore, when she entered the kitchen by the back door, she was humming a little tune to herself and smiling.

'Patrick!' she called. 'How are you, darling?'

She put the parcel down on the table and went through into the living-room; and when she saw him lying there on the floor with his legs doubled up and one arm twisted back underneath his body, it really was rather a shock. All the old love and longing for him welled up inside her, and she ran over to him, knelt down beside him, and began to cry her heart out. It was easy. No acting was necessary.

A few minutes later she got up and went to the phone. She knew the number of the police station, and when the man at the other end answered, she cried to him, 'Quick! Come quick! Patrick's dead!'

'Who's speaking?'

'Mrs Maloney. Mrs Patrick Maloney.'

'You mean Patrick Maloney's dead?'

'I think so,' she sobbed. 'He's lying on the floor and I think he's dead.'

'Be right over,' the man said.

The car came over quickly, and when she opened the front door, two policemen walked in. She knew them both – she knew nearly all the men at that precinct – and she fell right into Jack Noonan's arms, weeping hysterically. He put her gently into a chair, then went over to join the other one, who was called O'Malley, kneeling by the body.

'Is he dead?' she cried.

'I'm afraid he is. What happened?'

Briefly, she told her story about going out to the grocer and coming back to find him on the floor. While she was talking, crying and talking, Noonan discovered a small patch of congealed blood on the dead man's head. He showed it to O'Malley who got up at once and hurried to the phone.

Soon, other men began to come into the house. First a doctor, then two detectives, one of whom she knew by name. Later, a police photographer arrived and took pictures, and a man who knew about fingerprints. There was a great deal of whispering and muttering beside the corpse, and the detectives kept asking her a lot of questions. But they always treated her kindly. She told her story again, this time right from the beginning, when Patrick had come in, and she was sewing, and he was tired, so tired he hadn't wanted to go out for supper. She told how she'd put the meat in the oven – 'it's there now, cooking' – and how she'd slipped out to the grocer for vegetables, and come back to find him lying on the floor.

'Which grocer?' one of the detectives asked.

She told him, and he turned and whispered something to the other detective who immediately went outside into the street.

In fifteen minutes he was back with a page of notes, and there was more whispering, and through her sobbing she heard a few of the whispered phrases – '. . . acted quite normal . . . very cheerful . . . wanted to give him a good supper . . . peas . . . cheesecake . . . impossible that she . . .'

After a while, the photographer and the doctor departed and two other men came in and took the corpse away on a stretcher. Then the fingerprint man went away. The two detectives remained, and so did the two policemen. They were exceptionally nice to her, and Jack Noonan asked if she wouldn't rather go somewhere else, to her sister's house perhaps, or to his own wife who would take care of her and put her up for the night.

No, she said. She didn't feel she could move even a yard at the moment. Would they mind awfully if she stayed just where she was until she felt better? She didn't feel too good at the moment, she really didn't.

Then hadn't she better lie down on the bed? Jack Noonan asked.

No, she said, she'd like to stay right where she was, in this chair. A little later perhaps, when she felt better, she would move.

So they left her there while they went about their business, searching the house. Occasionally one of the detectives asked her another question. Sometimes Jack Noonan spoke to her gently as he passed by. Her husband, he told her, had been killed by a blow on the back of the head administered with a heavy blunt instrument, almost certainly a large piece of metal. They were looking for the weapon. The murderer may have taken it with him, but on the other hand he may've thrown it away or hidden it somewhere on the premises.

'It's the old story,' he said. 'Get the weapon, and you've got the man.'

Later, one of the detectives came up and sat beside her. Did she know, he asked, of anything in the house that could've been used as the weapon? Would she mind having a look around to see if anything was missing – a very big spanner for example, or a heavy metal vase.

They didn't have any heavy metal vases, she said.

'Or a big spanner?'

She didn't think they had a big spanner. But there might be some things like that in the garage.

The search went on. She knew that there were other policemen in the garden all around the house. She could hear their footsteps on the gravel outside, and sometimes she saw the flash of a torch through a chink in the curtains. It began to get late, nearly nine she noticed by the clock on the mantel. The four men searching the rooms seemed to be growing weary, a trifle exasperated.

'Jack,' she said, the next time Sergeant Noonan went by. 'Would you mind giving me a drink?'

'Sure I'll give you a drink. You mean this whisky?'

'Yes, please. But just a small one. It might make me feel better.'

He handed her the glass.

'Why don't you have one yourself,' she said. 'You must be awfully tired. Please do. You've been very good to me.'

'Well,' he answered. 'It's not strictly allowed, but I might take just a drop to keep me going.'

One by one the others came in and were persuaded to take a little nip of whisky. They stood around rather awkwardly with the drinks in their hands, uncomfortable in her presence, trying to say consoling things to her. Sergeant Noonan wandered into the kitchen, came out quickly and said, 'Look, Mrs Maloney. You know that oven of yours is still on, and the meat still inside.'

'Oh *dear* me!' she cried. 'So it is!'

'I better turn it off for you, hadn't I?'

'Will you do that, Jack? Thank you so much.'

When the sergeant returned the second time, she looked at him with her large, dark tearful eyes. 'Jack Noonan,' she said.

'Yes?'

'Would you do me a small favour – you and these others?'

 'We can try, Mrs Maloney.'

'Well,' she said. 'Here you all are, and good friends of dear Patrick's too, and helping to catch the man who killed him. You must be terribly hungry by now because it's long past your supper time, and I know Patrick would never forgive me, God bless his soul, if I allowed you to remain in his house without offering you decent hospitality. Why don't you eat up that lamb that's in the oven? It'll be cooked just right by now.'

'Wouldn't dream of it,' Sergeant Noonan said.

'Please,' she begged. 'Please eat it. Personally I couldn't touch a thing, certainly not what's been in the house when he was here. But it's all right for you. It'd be a favour to me if you'd eat it up. Then you can go on with your work again afterwards.'

There was a good deal of hesitating among the four policemen, but they were clearly hungry, and in the end they were persuaded to go into the kitchen and help themselves. The woman stayed where she was, listening to them through the open door, and she could hear them speaking among themselves, their voices thick and sloppy because their mouths were full of meat.

'Have some more, Charlie?'

'No. Better not finish it.'

'She *wants* us to finish it. She said so. Be doing her a favour.'

'Okay then. Give me some more.'

'That's the hell of a big club the guy must've used to hit poor Patrick,' one of them was saying. 'The doc says his skull was smashed all to pieces just like from a sledge-hammer.'

'That's why it ought to be easy to find.'

'Exactly what I say.'

'Whoever done it, they're not going to be carrying a thing like that around with them longer than they need.'

One of them belched.

'Personally, I think it's right here on the premises.'

'Probably right under our very noses. What you think, Jack?'

And in the other room, Mary Maloney began to giggle.

The Bookseller

If, in those days, you walked up from Trafalgar Square into Charing Cross Road, you would come in a few minutes to a shop on the right-hand side that had above the window the words WILLIAM BUGGAGE – RARE BOOKS.

If you peered through the window itself you would see that the walls were lined with books from floor to ceiling, and if you then pushed open the door and went in, you would immediately be assailed by that subtle odour of old cardboard and tea leaves that pervades the interiors of every second-hand bookshop in London. Nearly always, you would find two or three customers in there, silent shadowy figures in overcoats and trilby hats rummaging among the sets of Jane Austen and Trollope and Dickens and George Eliot, hoping to find a first edition.

No shop-keeper ever seemed to be hovering around to keep an eye on the customers, and if somebody actually wanted to pay for a book instead of pinching it and walking out, then he or she would have to push through a door at the back of the shop on which it said OFFICE – PAY HERE. If you went into the office you would find both Mr William Buggage and his assistant, Miss Muriel Tottle, seated at their respective desks and very much preoccupied.

Mr Buggage would be sitting behind a valuable eighteenth-century mahogany partner's desk, and Miss Tottle, a few feet away, would be using a somewhat smaller but no less elegant piece of furniture, a Regency writing-table with a top of faded green leather. On Mr Buggage's desk there would invariably be one copy of the day's London *Times*, as well as the *Daily Telegraph*, the *Manchester Guardian*, the *Western Mail*, and the *Glasgow Herald*. There would also be a current edition of *Who's Who* close at hand, fat and red and well thumbed. Miss Tottle's writing-table would have on it an electric typewriter and a plain but very nice open box containing notepaper and envelopes, as well as a quantity of paper-clips and staplers and other secretarial paraphernalia.

Now and again, but not very often, a customer would enter the office from the shop and would hand his chosen volume to Miss Tottle, who checked the price written in pencil on the fly-leaf and accepted the money, giving change when necessary from somewhere in the left-hand drawer of her writing-table. Mr Buggage never bothered even to glance up at those who came in and went out, and if one of them asked a question, it would be Miss Tottle who answered it.

Neither Mr Buggage nor Miss Tottle appeared to be in the least concerned about what went on in the main shop. In point of fact, Mr Buggage took the view that if someone was going to steal a book, then good luck to him. He knew very well that there was not a single valuable first edition out there on the shelves. There might be a moderately rare volume of Galsworthy or an early Waugh that had come in with a job lot bought at auction, and there were certainly some good sets of Boswell and Walter Scott and Robert Louis Stevenson and the rest, often very nicely bound in half or even whole calf. But those were not really the sort of things you could slip into your overcoat pocket. Even if a villain *did* walk out with half a dozen volumes, Mr Buggage wasn't going to lose any sleep over it. Why should he when he knew that the shop itself earned less money in a whole year than the back-room business grossed in a couple of days. It was what went on in the back room that counted.

One morning in February when the weather was foul and sleet was slanting white and wet on to the window-panes of the office, Mr Buggage and Miss Tottle were in their respective places as usual and each was engrossed, one might even say fascinated, by his and her own work. Mr Buggage, with a gold Parker pen poised above a note-pad, was reading *The Times* and jotting things down as he went along. Every now and again, he would refer to *Who's Who* and make more jottings.

Miss Tottle, who had been opening the mail, was now examining some cheques and adding up totals.

'Three today,' she said.

'What's it come to?' Mr Buggage asked, not looking up.

'One thousand six hundred,' Miss Tottle said.

Mr Buggage said, 'I don't suppose we've 'eard anything yet from that bishop's 'ouse in Chester, 'ave we?'

'A bishop lives in a palace, Billy, not a house,' Miss Tottle said.

'I don't give a sod where 'ee lives,' Mr Buggage said. 'But I get just a little bit uneasy when there's no quick answer from somebody like that.'

'As a matter of fact, the reply came this morning,' Miss Tottle said.

'Coughed up all right?'

'The full amount.'

'That's a relief,' Mr Buggage said. 'We never done a bishop before and I'm not sure it was any too clever.'

'The cheque came from some solicitors.'

Mr Buggage looked up sharply. 'Was there a letter?' he asked.

'Yes.'

'Read it.'

Miss Tottle found the letter and began to read: 'Dear Sir,

With reference to your communication of the 4th Instant, we enclose herewith a cheque for £537 in full settlement. Yours faithfully, Smithson, Briggs and Ellis.' Miss Tottle paused. 'That seems all right, doesn't it?'

'It's all right this time,' Mr Buggage said. 'But we don't want no more solicitors and let's not 'ave any more bishops either.'

'I agree about bishops,' Miss Tottle said. 'But you're not suddenly ruling out earls and lords and all that lot, I hope?'

'Lords is fine,' Mr Buggage said. 'We never 'ad no trouble with lords. Nor earls either. And didn't we do a duke once?'

'The Duke of Dorset,' Miss Tottle said. 'Did him last year. Over a thousand quid.'

'Very nice,' Mr Buggage said. 'I remember selectin' 'im myself straight off the front page.' He stopped talking while he prised a bit of food out from between two front teeth with the nail of his little finger. 'What I says is this,' he went on. 'The bigger the title, the bigger the twit. In fact, anyone's got a title on 'is name is almost certain to be a twit.'

'Now that's not quite true, Billy,' Miss Tottle said. 'Some people are given titles because they've done absolutely brilliant things, like inventing penicillin or climbing Mount Everest.'

'I'm talking about in'erited titles,' Mr Buggage said. 'Anyone gets born with a title, it's odds-on 'ee's a twit.'

'You're right there,' Miss Tottle said. 'We've never had the slightest trouble with the aristocracy.'

Mr Buggage leaned back in his chair and gazed solemnly at Miss Tottle. 'You know what?' he said. 'One of these days we might even 'ave a crack at royalty.'

'Ooh, I'd *love* it,' Miss Tottle said. 'Sock them for a fortune.'

Mr Buggage continued to gaze at Miss Tottle's profile, and as he did so, a slightly lascivious glint crept into his eye. One is forced to admit that Miss Tottle's appearance, when judged by the highest standards, was disappointing. To tell the truth when judged by *any* standards, it was still disappointing. Her face was long and horsey and her teeth, which were also rather long, had a sulphurous tinge about them. So did her skin. The best you could say about her was that she had a generous bosom, but even that had its faults. It was the kind that makes a single long tightly bound bulge from one side of the chest to the other, and at first glance one got the impression that there were not two individual breasts growing out of her body but simply one big long loaf of bread.

Then again, Mr Buggage himself was in no position to be overly finicky. When one saw him for the first time, the word that sprang instantly to mind was 'grubby'. He was squat, paunchy, bald and flaccid, and so far as his face was concerned, one could only make a guess at what it looked like because not much of it was visible to the eye. The major part was covered over by an immense thicket of black, bushy, slightly curly hair, a fashion, one fears, that is all too common these days, a foolish practice and incidentally a rather dirty habit. Why so many males wish to conceal their facial characteristics is beyond the comprehension of us ordinary mortals. One must presume that if it were possible for these people also to grow hair all over their noses and cheeks and eyes, then they would do so, ending up with no visible face at all but only an obscene and rather gamey ball of hair. The only possible conclusion one can arrive at when looking at one of these bearded males is that the vegetation is a kind of smoke-screen and is cultivated in order to conceal something unsightly or unsavoury.

This was almost certainly true in Mr Buggage's case, and it was therefore fortunate for all of us, and especially for Miss

Tottle, that the beard was there. Mr Buggage continued to gaze wistfully at his assistant. Then he said, 'Now pet, why don't you 'urry up and get them cheques in the post because after you've done that I've got a little proposal to put to you.'

Miss Tottle looked back over her shoulder at the speaker and gave him a smirk that showed the cutting edges of her sulphur teeth. Whenever he called her 'pet', it was a sure sign that feelings of a carnal nature were beginning to stir within Mr Buggage's breast, and in other parts as well.

'Tell it to me now, lover,' she said.

'You get them cheques done first,' he said. He could be very commanding at times, and Miss Tottle thought it was wonderful.

Miss Tottle now began what she called her Daily Audit. This involved examining all of Mr Buggage's bank accounts and all of her own and then deciding into which of them the latest cheques should be paid. Mr Buggage, you see, at this particular moment, had exactly sixty-six different accounts in his own name and Miss Tottle had twenty-two. These were scattered around among various branches of the big three banks, Barclays, Lloyds, and National Westminster, all over London and a few in the suburbs. There was nothing wrong with that. And it had not been difficult, as the business became more and more successful, for either of them to walk into any branch of these banks and open a Current Account, with an initial deposit of a few hundred pounds. They would then receive a cheque book, a paying-in book and the promise of a monthly statement.

Mr Buggage had discovered early on that if a person has an account with several or even many different branches of a bank, this will cause no comment by the staff. Each branch deals

strictly with its own customers and their names are not circulated to other branches or to Head Office, not even in these computerized times.

On the other hand, banks are required by law to notify the Inland Revenue of the names of all clients who have Deposit Accounts containing one thousand pounds or more. They must also report the amounts of interest earned. But no such law applies to Current Accounts because they earn no interest. Nobody takes any notice of a person's Current Account unless it is overdrawn or unless, and this seldom happens, the balance becomes ridiculously large. A Current Account containing let us say £100,000 might easily raise an eyebrow or two among the staff, and the client would almost certainly get a nice letter from the manager suggesting that some of the money be placed on deposit to earn interest. But Mr Buggage didn't give a fig for interest and he wanted no raised eyebrows either. That is why he and Miss Tottle had eighty-eight different bank accounts between them. It was Miss Tottle's job to see that the amounts in each of these accounts never exceeded £20,000. Anything more than that might, in Mr Buggage's opinion, cause an eyebrow to raise, especially if it were left lying untouched in a Current Account for months or years. The agreement between the two partners was seventy-five per cent of the profits of the business to Mr Buggage and twenty-five per cent to Miss Tottle.

Miss Tottle's Daily Audit involved examining a list she kept of all the balances in all those eighty-eight separate accounts and then deciding into which of them the daily cheque or cheques should be deposited. She had in her filing-cabinet eighty-eight different files, one for each bank account, and eighty-eight different cheque books and eighty-eight different paying-in books. Miss Tottle's task was not a complicated one but she had to keep her wits about her and not muddle things up. Only the previous week they had to open four new accounts at four new branches, three for Mr Buggage and one for Miss Tottle. 'Soon we're goin' to 'ave over a 'undred accounts in our names,' Mr Buggage had said to Miss Tottle at the time.

'Why not two hundred?' Miss Tottle had said.

'A day will come,' Mr Buggage said, 'when we'll 'ave used up all the banks in this part of the country and you and I is goin' to 'ave to travel all the way up to Sunderland or Newcastle to open new ones.'

But now Miss Tottle was busy with her Daily Audit. 'That's done,' she said, putting the last cheque and the paying-in slip into its envelope.

''Ow much we got in our accounts all together at this very moment?' Mr Buggage asked her.

Miss Tottle unlocked the middle drawer of her writing-table and took out a plain school exercise book. On the cover she had written the words *My old arithmetic book from school.* She considered this a rather ingenious ploy designed to put people off the scent should the book ever fall into the wrong hands. 'Just let me add on today's deposit,' she said, finding the right page and beginning to write down figures. 'There we are. Counting today, *you* have got in all the sixty-six branches, one million, three hundred and twenty thousand, six hundred and forty-three pounds, unless you've been cashing any cheques in the last few days.'

'I 'aven't,' Mr Buggage said. 'And what've you got?'

'*I* have got . . . four hundred and thirty thousand, seven hundred and twenty-five pounds.'

'Very nice,' Mr Buggage said. 'And 'ow long's it taken us to gather in those tidy little sums?'

'Just eleven years,' Miss Tottle said. 'What was that teeny weeny proposal you were going to put to me, lover?'

'Ah,' Mr Buggage said, laying down his gold pencil and leaning back to gaze at her once again with that pale licentious eye. 'I was just thinkin' . . . 'ere's exactly what I was thinkin' . . . why on earth should a millionaire like me be sittin' 'ere in this filthy freezin' weather when I could be reclinin' in the lap of luxury beside a swimmin' pool with a nice girl like you to keep me company and flunkeys bringin' us goblets of iced champagne every few minutes?'

'Why indeed?' Miss Tottle cried, grinning widely.

'Then get out the book and let's see where we 'aven't been.'

Miss Tottle walked over to a bookshelf on the opposite wall and took down a thickish paperback called *The 300 Best Hotels in the World chosen by René Lecler.* She returned to her chair and said, 'Where to this time, lover?'

'Somewhere in North Africa,' Mr Buggage said. 'This is February and you've got to go at least to North Africa to get it really warm. Italy's not 'ot enough yet, nor is Spain. And I don't want the flippin' West Indies. I've 'ad enough of them. Where 'aven't we been in North Africa?'

Miss Tottle was turning the pages of the book. 'That's not so easy,' she said. 'We've done the Palais Jamai in Fez . . . and the Gazelle d'Or in Taroudant . . . and the Tunis Hilton in Tunis. We didn't like that one . . .'

''Ow many we done so far altogether in that book?' Mr Buggage asked her.

'I think it was forty-eight the last time I counted.'

'And I 'as every intention of doin' all three 'undred of 'em before I'm finished,' Mr Buggage said. 'That's my big ambition and I'll bet nobody else 'as ever done it.'

'I think Mr René Lecler must have done it,' Miss Tottle said.

''Oo's 'ee?'

'The man who wrote the book.'

''Ee don't count,' Mr Buggage said. He leaned sideways in his chair and began to scratch the left cheek of his rump in a slow meditative manner. 'And I'll bet 'ee 'asn't anyway. These travel guides use any Tom, Dick and 'Arry to go round for 'em.'

'Here's one!' Miss Tottle cried. 'Hotel La Mamounia in Marrakech.'

'Where's that?'

'In Morocco. Just round the top corner of Africa on the left-hand side.'

'Go on then. What does it say about it?'

'It says,' Miss Tottle read, '*This was Winston Churchill's favourite haunt and from his balcony he painted the Atlas sunset time and again.*'

'I don't paint,' Mr Buggage said. 'What else does it say?'

Miss Tottle read on: '*As the liveried Moorish servant shows you into the tiled and latticed colonnaded court, you step decisively into an illustration of the 1001 Arabian nights . . .*'

'That's more like it,' Mr Buggage said. 'Go on.'

'*Your next contact with reality will come when you pay your bill on leaving.*'

'That don't worry us millionaires,' Mr Buggage said. 'Let's go. We'll leave tomorrow. Call that travel agent right away. First class. We'll shut the shop for ten days.'

'Don't you want to do today's letters?'

'Bugger today's letters,' Mr Buggage said. 'We're on 'oliday from now on. Get on to that travel agent quick.' He leaned the other way now and started scratching his right buttock with the fingers of his right hand. Miss Tottle watched him and Mr

Buggage saw her watching him but he didn't care. 'Call that travel agent,' he said.

'And I'd better get us some Travellers Cheques,' Miss Tottle said.

'Get five thousand quids' worth. I'll write the cheque. This one's on me. Give me a cheque book. Choose the nearest bank. And call that 'otel in wherever it was and ask for the biggest suite they've got. They're never booked up when you want the biggest suite.'

Twenty-four hours later, Mr Buggage and Miss Tottle were sun-bathing beside the pool at La Mamounia in Marrakech and they were drinking champagne.

'This is the life,' Miss Tottle said. 'Why don't we retire altogether and buy a grand house in a climate like this?'

'What do we want to retire for?' Mr Buggage said. 'We got the best business in London goin' for us and personally I find that very enjoyable.'

On the other side of the pool a dozen Moroccan servants were laying out a splendid buffet lunch for the guests. There were enormous cold lobsters and large pink hams and very small roast chickens and several kinds of rice and about ten different salads. A chef was grilling steaks over a charcoal fire. Guests were beginning to get up from deck-chairs and mattresses to mill around the buffet with plates in their hands. Some were in swimsuits, some in light summer clothes, and most had straw hats on their heads. Mr Buggage was watching them. Almost without exception, they were English. They were the very rich English, smooth, well mannered, overweight, loud-voiced and infinitely dull. He had seen them before all around Jamaica and Barbados and places like that. It was evident that quite a few of them knew one another because at home, of course, they moved in the same circles. But whether they knew each other or not, they certainly *accepted* each other because all of them belonged to the same nameless and exclusive club. Any member of this club could always, by some subtle social alchemy, recognize a fellow member at a glance. Yes, they say to themselves, he's one of us. She's one of us. Mr Buggage was not one of them. He was not in the club and he never would be. He was a *nouveau* and that, regardless of how many millions he had, was unacceptable. He was also overtly vulgar and that was unacceptable, too. The very rich could be just as vulgar as Mr Buggage, or even more so, but they did it in a different way.

'There they are,' Mr Buggage said, looking across the pool at the guests. 'Them's our bread and butter. Every one of 'em's likely to be a future customer.'

'How right you are,' Miss Tottle said.

Mr Buggage, lying on a mattress that was striped in blue, red, and green, was propped up on one elbow, staring at the guests. His stomach was bulging out in folds over his swimming-trunks and droplets of sweat were running out of the fatty crevices. Now he shifted his gaze to the recumbent figure of Miss Tottle lying beside him on her own mattress. Miss Tottle's loaf-of-bread bosom was encased in a strip of scarlet bikini. The bottom half of the bikini was daringly brief and possibly a shade too small and Mr Buggage could see traces of black hair high up on the inside of her thighs.

'We'll 'ave our lunch, pet, then we'll go to our room and take a little nap, right?'

Miss Tottle displayed her sulphurous teeth and nodded her head.

'And after that we'll do some letters.'

'Letters?' she cried. 'I don't want to do letters! I thought this was going to be a holiday!'

‘It *is* a ’oliday, pet, but I don’t like lettin’ good business go to waste. The ’otel will lend you a typewriter. I already checked on that. And they’re lendin’ me their *’Oo’s ’Oo*. Every good ’otel in the world keeps an English *’Oo’s ’Oo.* The manager likes to know ’oo’s important so ’ee can kiss their backsides.’

‘They won’t find *you* in it,’ Miss Tottle said, a bit huffy now.

‘No,’ Mr Buggage said. ‘I’ll grant you that. But they won’t find many in it that’s got more money’n me neither. In this world, it’s not ’oo you are, my girl. It’s not even ’oo you know. It’s what you *got* that counts.’

‘We’ve never done letters on holiday before,’ Miss Tottle said.

‘There’s a first time for everything, pet.’

‘How can we do letters without newspapers?’

‘You know very well English papers always go airmail to places like this. I bought a *Times* in the foyer when we arrived. It’s actually the same as I was workin’ on in the office yesterday so I done most of my ’omework already. I’m beginning to fancy a piece of that lobster over there. You ever seen bigger lobsters than that?’

‘But you’re surely not going to *post* the letters from here, are you?’ Miss Tottle said.

‘Certainly not. We’ll leave ’em undated and date ’em and post ’em as soon as we return. That way we’ll ’ave a nice backlog up our sleeves.’

Miss Tottle stared at the lobsters on the table across the pool, then at the people milling around, then she reached out and placed a hand on Mr Buggage’s thigh, high up under the bathing-shorts. She began to stroke the hairy thigh. ‘Come on, Billy,’ she said, ‘why don’t we take a break from the letters same as we always do when we’re on hols?’

‘You surely don’t want us throwing about a thousand quid

away a day, do you?' Mr Buggage said. 'And quarter of it yours, don't forget that.'

'We don't have the firm's notepaper and we can't use hotel paper, for God's sake.'

'I brought the notepaper,' Mr Buggage said, triumphant. 'I got a 'ole box of it. *And* envelopes.'

'Oh, all *right*,' Miss Tottle said. 'Are you going to fetch me some of that lobster, lover?'

'We'll go together,' Mr Buggage said, and he stood up and started waddling round the pool in those almost knee-length bathing-trunks he had bought a couple of years back in Honolulu. They had a pattern of green and yellow and white flowers on them. Miss Tottle got to her feet and followed him.

Mr Buggage was busy helping himself at the buffet when he heard a man's voice behind him saying, 'Fiona, I don't think you've met Mrs Smith-Swithin . . . and this is Lady Hedgecock.'

'How d'you do' . . . 'How d'you do,' the voices said.

Mr Buggage glanced round at the speakers. There was a man and a woman in swimming-clothes and two elderly ladies wearing cotton dresses. Those names, he thought. I've heard those names before, I know I have . . . Smith-Swithin . . . Lady Hedgecock. He shrugged and continued to load food on to his plate.

A few minutes later, he was sitting with Miss Tottle at a small table under a sun-umbrella and each of them was tucking into an immense half lobster. 'Tell me, does the name Lady 'Edgecock mean anything to you?' Mr Buggage asked, talking with his mouth full.

'Lady Hedgecock? She's one of our clients. Or she was. I never forget names like that. Why?'

'And what about a Mrs Smith-Swithin? Does that also ring a bell?'

'It does, actually,' Miss Tottle said. 'Both of them do. Why do you ask that suddenly?'

'Because both of 'em's 'ere.'

'Good God! How d'you know?'

'And what's more, my girl, they're together! They're chums!'

'They're not!'

'Oh, yes they are!'

Mr Buggage told her how he knew. 'There they are,' he said, pointing with a fork whose prongs were yellow with mayonnaise. 'Those two fat old broads talkin' to the tall man and the woman.'

Miss Tottle stared, fascinated. 'You know,' she said, 'I've never *actually* seen a client of ours in the flesh before, not in all the years we've been in business.'

'Nor me,' Mr Buggage said. 'One thing's for sure. I picked 'em right, didn't I? They're rolling in it. That's obvious. And they're stupid. That's even more obvious.'

'Do you think it could be dangerous, Billy, the two of them knowing each other?'

'It's a bloody queer coincidence,' Mr Buggage said, 'but I don't think it's dangerous. Neither of 'em's ever goin' to say a word. That's the beauty of it.'

'I guess you're right.'

'The only possible danger,' Mr Buggage said, 'would be if they saw my name on the register. I got a very unusual name just like theirs. It would ring bells at once.'

'Guests don't see the register,' Miss Tottle said.

'No, they don't,' Mr Buggage said. 'No one's ever goin' to bother us. They never 'as and they never will.'

'Amazing lobster,' Miss Tottle said.

'Lobster is sex food,' Mr Buggage announced, eating more of it.

'You're thinking of oysters, lover.'

'I am not thinking of oysters. Oysters is sex food, too, but lobsters is stronger. A dish of lobsters can drive some people crazy.'

'Like you, perhaps?' she said, wriggling her rump in the chair.

'Maybe,' Mr Buggage said. 'We shall just 'ave to wait and see about that, won't we, pet?'

'Yes,' she said.

'It's a good thing they're so expensive,' Mr Buggage said. 'If every Tom, Dick and 'Arry could afford to buy 'em, the 'ole world would be full of *sex maniacs*.'

'Keep eating it,' she said.

After lunch, the two of them went upstairs to their suite, where they cavorted clumsily on the huge bed for a brief period. Then they took a nap.

And now they were in their private sitting-room and were wearing only dressing-gowns over their nakedness, Mr Buggage in a plum-coloured silk one, Miss Tottle in pastel pink and pale green. Mr Buggage was reclining on the sofa with a copy of yesterday's *Times* on his lap and a *Who's Who* on the coffee table.

Miss Tottle was at the writing-desk with a hotel typewriter before her and a notebook in her hand. Both were again drinking champagne.

'This is a prime one,' Mr Buggage was saying. 'Sir Edward Leishman. Got the lead obit. Chairman of Aerodynamics Engineering. *One of our major industrialists*, it says.'

'Nice,' Miss Tottle said. 'Make sure the wife's alive.'

'*Leaves a widow and three children*,' Mr Buggage read out. 'And . . . wait a minute . . . in *'Oo's 'Oo* it says, *Recreations, walkin' and fishin'. Clubs, White's and the Reform.*'

'Address?' Miss Tottle asked.

'The Red House, Andover, Wilts.'

'How d'you spell Leishman?' Miss Tottle asked. Mr Buggage spelled it.

'How much shall we go for?'

'A lot,' Mr Buggage said. 'He was loaded. Try around nine 'undred.'

'You want to slip in *The Compleat Angler*? It says he was a fisherman.'

'Yes. First edition. Four 'undred and twenty quid. You know the rest of it by 'eart. Bang it out quick. I got another good one to come.'

Miss Tottle put a sheet of notepaper into the typewriter and very rapidly she began to type. She had done so many thousands of these letters over the years that she never had to pause for one word. She even knew how to compile the list of books so that it came out to around nine hundred pounds or three hundred and fifty pounds or five hundred and twenty or whatever. She could make it come out to any sum Mr Buggage thought the client would stand. One of the secrets of this particular trade, as Mr Buggage knew, was never to be too greedy. Never go over a thousand quid with anyone, not even a famous millionaire.

The letter, as Miss Tottle typed it, went like this:

WILLIAM BUGGAGE – RARE BOOKS

27a Charing Cross Road
London.

Dear Lady Leishman,

It is with very great regret that I trouble you at this tragic time of your bereavement, but regretfully I am left with no alternative in the circumstances.

I had the pleasure of serving your late husband over a number of years and my invoices were always sent to him care of White's Club, as indeed were many of the little parcels of books that he collected with such enthusiasm.

He was always a prompt settler and a very pleasant gentleman to deal with. I am listing below his more recent purchases, those which, alas, he had ordered in more recent times before he passed away and which were delivered to him in the usual manner.

Perhaps I should explain to you that publications of this nature are often very rare and can therefore be rather costly. Some are privately printed, some are actually banned in this country and those are more costly still.

Rest assured, dear madam, that I always conduct business in the strictest confidence. My own reputation over many years in the trade is the best guarantee of my discretion. When the bill is paid, that is the last you will hear of the matter, unless of course you happen to be able to lay hands on your late husband's collection of erotica, in which case I should be happy to make you an offer for it.

To Books:

THE COMPLEAT ANGLER, Isaak Walton, First Edition. Good clean copy. Some rubbing of edges. Rare.	£420
LOVE IN FURS, Leopold von Sacher-Masoch, 1920 edition. Slip cover.	75
SEXUAL SECRETS, Translated from Danish.	40
HOW TO PLEASURE YOUNG GIRLS WHEN YOU ARE OVER SIXTY, Illustrations. Private printing from Paris.	95
THE ART OF PUNISHMENT – THE CANE, THE WHIP AND THE LASH, Translated from German. Banned in U.K.	115
THREE NAUGHTY NUNS, Good clean edition.	60
RESTRAINT – SHACKLES AND SILKEN CORDS, Illustrations.	80
WHY TEENAGERS PREFER OLD MEN, Illustrations. American.	90

THE LONDON DIRECTORY OF ESCORTS AND HOSTESSES, Current edition. 20

Total now due £995

Yours faithfully,
William Buggage

'Right,' Miss Tottle said, running the notepaper out of her typewriter. 'Done that one. But you realize I don't have my "Bible" here, so I'll have to check the names when I get home before posting the letters.'

'You do that,' Mr Buggage said.

Miss Tottle's Bible was a massive index-card file in which were recorded the names and addresses of every client they had written to since the beginning of the business. The purpose of this was to try as nearly as possible to ensure that no two members of the same family received a Buggage invoice. If this were to happen, there would always be the danger that they might compare notes. It also served to guard against a case where a widow who had received one invoice upon the death of her first husband might be sent another invoice on the death of the second husband. That, of course, would let the cat right out of the bag. There was no guaranteed way of avoiding this perilous mistake because the widow would have changed her name when she remarried, but Miss Tottle had developed an instinct for sniffing out such pitfalls, and the Bible helped her to do it.

'What's next?' Miss Tottle asked.

'The next is Major General Lionel Anstruther. Here 'ee is. Got about six inches in *'Oo's 'Oo. Clubs, Army and Navy. Recreations, Ridin' to 'Ounds.*'

'I suppose he fell off a horse and broke his flipping neck,'

Miss Tottle said. 'I'll start with *Memoirs of a Foxhunting Man, first edition*, right?'

'Right. Two 'undred and twenty quid,' Mr Buggage said. 'And make it between five and six 'undred altogether.'

'Okay.'

'And put in *The Sting of the Ridin' Crop.* Whips seem to come natural to these fox-huntin' folk.'

And so it went on.

The holiday in Marrakech continued pleasantly enough and nine days later Mr Buggage and Miss Tottle were back in the office in Charing Cross Road, both with sun-scorched skins as red as the shells of the many lobsters they had eaten. They quickly settled down again into their normal and stimulating routine. Day after day the letters went out and the cheques came in. It was remarkable how smoothly the business ran. The psychology behind it was, of course, very sound. Strike a widow at the height of her grief, strike her with something that is unbearably awful, something she wants to forget about and put behind her, something she wants nobody else to discover. What's more, the funeral is imminent. So she pays up fast to get the sordid little business out of the way. Mr Buggage knew his onions. In all the years he had been operating, he had never once had a protest or an angry reply. Just a cheque in an envelope. Now and again, but not often, there was no reply at all. The disbelieving widow had been brave enough to sling his letter into the waste-paper basket and that was the end of it. None of them quite dared to challenge the invoice because they could never be absolutely positive that the late husband had been as pure as the wife believed and hoped. Men never are. In many cases, of course, the widow knew very well that her beloved had been a lecherous old bird and Mr Buggage's invoice came as no surprise. So she paid up even faster.

About a month after their return from Marrakech, on a wet and rainy afternoon in March, Mr Buggage was reclining comfortably in his office with his feet up on the top of his fine partner's desk, dictating to Miss Tottle some details about a deceased and distinguished admiral. '*Recreations*,' he was saying, reading from *Who's Who*, '*gardening, sailing and stamp-collecting* . . .' At that point, the door from the main shop opened and a young man came in with a book in his hand. 'Mr Buggage?' he said.

Mr Buggage looked up. 'Over there,' he said, waving towards Miss Tottle. 'She'll deal with you.'

The young man stood still. His navy-blue overcoat was wet from the weather and droplets of water were dripping from his hair. He didn't look at Miss Tottle. He kept his eyes on Mr Buggage. 'Don't you want the money?' he said, pleasantly enough.

'She'll take it.'

'Why won't you take it?'

'Because she's the cashier,' Mr Buggage said. 'You want to buy a book, go ahead. She'll deal with you.'

'I'd rather deal with *you*,' the young man said.

Mr Buggage looked up at him. 'Go on,' he said. 'Just do as you're told, there's a good lad.'

'You *are* the proprietor?' the young man said. 'You *are* Mr William Buggage?'

'What if I am,' Mr Buggage said, his feet still up on the desk.

'Are you or aren't you?'

'What's it to you?' Mr Buggage said.

'So that's settled,' the young man said. 'How d'you do, Mr Buggage.' There was a curious edge to his voice now, a mixture of scorn and mockery.

Mr Buggage took his feet down from the desk-top and sat up

a trifle straighter. 'You're a bit of a cheeky young bugger, aren't you?' he said. 'If you want that book I suggest you just pay your money over there and then you can 'op it. Right?'

The young man turned towards the still open door that led to the front of the shop. Just the other side of the door there were a couple of the usual kind of customers, men in raincoats, pulling out books and examining them.

'Mother,' the young man called softly. 'You can come in, Mother. Mr Buggage is here.'

A small woman of about sixty came in and stood beside the young man. She had a trim figure for her age and a face that must once have been ravishing, but now it showed traces of strain and exhaustion, and the pale blue eyes were dulled with grief. She was wearing a black coat and a simple black hat. She left the door open behind her.

'Mr Buggage,' the young man said. 'This is my mother, Mrs Northcote.'

Miss Tottle, the rememberer of names, turned round quick and looked at Mr Buggage and made little warning movements with her mouth. Mr Buggage got the message and said as politely as he could, 'And what can I do for you, madam?'

The woman opened her black handbag and took out a letter. She unfolded it carefully and held it out to Mr Buggage. 'Then it will be you who sent me this?' she said.

Mr Buggage took the letter and examined it at some length. Miss Tottle, who had turned right round in her chair now, was watching Mr Buggage.

'Yes,' Mr Buggage said. 'This is my letter and my invoice. All correct and in order. What is your problem, madam?'

'What I came here to ask you,' the woman said, 'is, are you sure it's right?'

'I'm afraid it is, madam.'

'But it is so unbelievable . . . I find it impossible to believe that my husband bought those books.'

'Let's see now, your 'usband, Mr . . . Mr . . . er . . .'

'Northcote,' Miss Tottle said.

'Yes, Mr Northcote, yes, of course, Mr Northcote. 'Ee wasn't in 'ere often, once or twice a year maybe, but a good customer and a very fine gentleman. May I offer you, madam, my sincere condolences on your sad loss.'

'Thank you, Mr Buggage. But are you really quite certain you haven't been mixing him up with somebody else?'

'Not a chance, madam. Not the slightest chance. My good secretary over there will confirm that there is no mistake.'

'May I see it?' Miss Tottle said, getting up and crossing to take the letter from Mr Buggage. 'Yes,' she said, examining it. 'I typed this myself. There is no mistake.'

'Miss Tottle's been with me a long time,' Mr Buggage said. 'She knows the business inside out. I can't remember 'er ever makin' a mistake.'

'I should hope not,' Miss Tottle said.

'So there you are, madam,' Mr Buggage said.

'It simply isn't *possible*,' the woman said.

'Ah, but men will be men,' Mr Buggage said. 'They all 'ave their little bit of fun now and again and there's no 'arm in that, is there, madam?' He sat confident and unmoved in his chair, waiting now to have done with it. He felt himself master of the situation.

The woman stood very straight and still, and she was looking Mr Buggage directly in the eyes. 'These curious books you list on your invoice,' she said, 'do they print them in Braille?'

'In what?'

'In Braille.'

'I don't know what you're talking about, madam.'

'I thought you wouldn't,' she said. 'That's the only way my husband could have read them. He lost his sight in the last war, in the Battle of Alamein more than forty years ago, and he was blind for ever after.'

The office became suddenly very quiet. The mother and her son stood motionless, watching Mr Buggage. Miss Tottle turned away and looked out of the window. Mr Buggage cleared his throat as though to say something, but thought better of it. The two men in raincoats, who were close enough to have heard every word through the open door, came quietly into the office. One of them held out a plastic card and said to Mr Buggage, 'Inspector Richards, Serious Crimes Division, Scotland Yard.' And to Miss Tottle, who was already moving back towards her desk, he said, 'Don't touch any of those papers, please miss. Leave everything just where it is. You're both coming along with us.'

The son took his mother gently by the arm and led her out of the office, through the shop and on to the street.

The Butler

As soon as George Cleaver had made his first million, he and Mrs Cleaver moved out of their small suburban villa into an elegant London house. They acquired a French chef called Monsieur Estragon and an English butler called Tibbs, both wildly expensive. With the help of these two experts, the Cleavers set out to climb the social ladder and began to give dinner parties several times a week on a lavish scale.

But these dinners never seemed quite to come off. There was no animation, no spark to set the conversation alight, no style at all. Yet the food was superb and the service faultless.

'What the heck's wrong with our parties, Tibbs?' Mr Cleaver said to the butler. 'Why don't nobody never loosen up and let themselves go?'

Tibbs inclined his head to one side and looked at the ceiling. 'I hope, sir, you will not be offended if I offer a small suggestion.'

'What is it?'

'It's the wine, sir.'

'What about the wine?'

'Well, sir, Monsieur Estragon serves superb food. Superb food should be accompanied by superb wine. But you serve them a cheap and very odious Spanish red.'

'Then why in heaven's name didn't you say so before, you twit?' cried Mr Cleaver. 'I'm not short of money. I'll give them the best flipping wine in the world if that's what they want! What *is* the best wine in the world?'

'Claret, sir,' the butler replied, 'from the greatest *châteaux* in Bordeaux – Lafite, Latour, Haut-Brion, Margaux, Mouton-Rothschild and Cheval Blanc. And from only the very greatest vintage years, which are, in my opinion, 1906, 1914, 1929 and 1945. Cheval Blanc was also magnificent in 1895 and 1921, and Haut-Brion in 1906.'

'Buy them all!' said Mr Cleaver. 'Fill the flipping cellar from top to bottom!'

'I can try, sir,' the butler said. 'But wines like these are extremely rare and cost a fortune.'

'I don't give a hoot what they cost!' said Mr Cleaver. 'Just go out and get them!'

That was easier said than done. Nowhere in England or in France could Tibbs find any wine from 1895, 1906, 1914 or 1921. But he did manage to get hold of some twenty-nines and forty-fives. The bills for these wines were astronomical. They were in fact so huge that even Mr Cleaver began to sit up and take notice. And his interest quickly turned into outright enthusiasm when the butler suggested to him that a knowledge of wine was a very considerable social asset. Mr Cleaver bought books on the subject and read them from cover to cover. He also learned a great deal from Tibbs himself, who taught him, among other things, just how wine should be properly tasted. 'First, sir, you sniff it long and deep, with your nose right inside the top of the glass, like this. Then you take a mouthful and you open your lips a tiny bit and suck in air, letting the air bubble through the wine. Watch me do it. Then you roll it vigorously around your mouth. And finally you swallow it.'

In due course, Mr Cleaver came to regard himself as an expert on wine, and inevitably he turned into a colossal bore.

'Ladies and gentlemen,' he would announce at dinner, holding up his glass, 'this is a Margaux '29! The greatest year of the century! Fantastic bouquet! Smells of cowslips! And notice especially the after taste and how the tiny trace of tannin gives it that glorious astringent quality! Terrific, ain't it?'

The guests would nod and sip and mumble a few praises, but that was all.

'What's the matter with the silly twerps?' Mr Cleaver said to Tibbs after this had gone on for some time. 'Don't none of them appreciate a great wine?'

The butler laid his head to one side and gazed upward. 'I think they *would* appreciate it, sir,' he said, 'if they were able to taste it. But they can't.'

'What the heck d'you mean, they can't taste it?'

'I believe, sir, that you have instructed Monsieur Estragon to put liberal quantities of vinegar in the salad-dressing.'

'What's wrong with that? I like vinegar.'

'Vinegar,' the butler said, 'is the enemy of wine. It destroys the palate. The dressing should be made of pure olive oil and a little lemon juice. Nothing else.'

'Hogwash!' said Mr Cleaver.

'As you wish, sir.'

'I'll say it again, Tibbs. You're talking hogwash. The vinegar don't spoil my palate one bit.'

'You are very fortunate, sir,' the butler murmured, backing out of the room.

That night at dinner, the host began to mock his butler in front of the guests. 'Mister Tibbs,' he said, 'has been trying to tell me I can't taste my wine if I put vinegar in the salad-dressing. Right, Tibbs?'

'Yes, sir,' Tibbs replied gravely.

'And I told him hogwash. Didn't I, Tibbs?'

'Yes, sir.'

'This wine,' Mr Cleaver went on, raising his glass, 'tastes to me exactly like a Château Lafite '45, and what's more it is a Château Lafite '45.'

Tibbs, the butler, stood very still and erect near the sideboard, his face pale. 'If you'll forgive me, sir,' he said, 'that is not a Lafite '45.'

Mr Cleaver swung round in his chair and stared at the butler. 'What the heck d'you mean,' he said. 'There's the empty bottles beside you to prove it!'

These great clarets, being old and full of sediment, were always decanted by Tibbs before dinner. They were served in cut-glass decanters, while the empty bottles, as is the custom, were placed on the sideboard. Right now, two empty bottles of Lafite '45 were standing on the sideboard for all to see.

'The wine you are drinking, sir,' the butler said quietly, 'happens to be that cheap and rather odious Spanish red.'

Mr Cleaver looked at the wine in his glass, then at the butler. The blood was coming to his face now, his skin was turning scarlet. 'You're lying, Tibbs!' he said.

'No sir, I'm not lying,' the butler said. 'As a matter of fact, I have never served you any other wine but Spanish red since I've been here. It seemed to suit you very well.'

'I don't believe him!' Mr Cleaver cried out to his guests. 'The man's gone mad.'

'Great wines,' the butler said, 'should be treated with reverence. It is bad enough to destroy the palate with three or four cocktails before dinner, as you people do, but when you slosh vinegar over your food into the bargain, then you might just as well be drinking dishwater.'

Ten outraged faces around the table stared at the butler. He had caught them off-balance. They were speechless.

'This,' the butler said, reaching out and touching one of the empty bottles lovingly with his fingers, 'this is the last of the forty-fives. The twenty-nines have already been finished. But they were glorious wines. Monsieur Estragon and I enjoyed them immensely.'

The butler bowed and walked quite slowly from the room. He crossed the hall and went out of the front door of the house into the street where Monsieur Estragon was already loading their suitcases into the boot of the small car which they owned together.

PENGUIN 60s

MARTIN AMIS · *God's Dice*
HANS CHRISTIAN ANDERSEN · *The Emperor's New Clothes*
MARCUS AURELIUS · *Meditations*
JAMES BALDWIN · *Sonny's Blues*
AMBROSE BIERCE · *An Occurrence at Owl Creek Bridge*
DIRK BOGARDE · *From Le Pigeonnier*
WILLIAM BOYD · *Killing Lizards*
POPPY Z. BRITE · *His Mouth will Taste of Wormwood*
ITALO CALVINO · *Ten Italian Folktales*
ALBERT CAMUS · *Summer*
TRUMAN CAPOTE · *First and Last*
RAYMOND CHANDLER · *Goldfish*
ANTON CHEKHOV · *The Black Monk*
ROALD DAHL · *Lamb to the Slaughter*
ELIZABETH DAVID · *I'll be with You in the Squeezing of a Lemon*
N. J. DAWOOD (TRANS.) · *The Seven Voyages of Sindbad the Sailor*
ISAK DINESEN · *The Dreaming Child*
SIR ARTHUR CONAN DOYLE · *The Man with the Twisted Lip*
DICK FRANCIS · *Racing Classics*
SIGMUND FREUD · *Five Lectures on Psycho-Analysis*
KAHLIL GIBRAN · *Prophet, Madman, Wanderer*
STEPHEN JAY GOULD · *Adam's Navel*
ALASDAIR GRAY · *Five Letters from an Eastern Empire*
GRAHAM GREENE · *Under the Garden*
JAMES HERRIOT · *Seven Yorkshire Tales*
PATRICIA HIGHSMITH · *Little Tales of Misogyny*
M. R. JAMES AND R. L. STEVENSON · *The Haunted Dolls' House*
RUDYARD KIPLING · *Baa Baa, Black Sheep*
PENELOPE LIVELY · *A Long Night at Abu Simbel*
KATHERINE MANSFIELD · *The Escape*

PENGUIN 60s

GABRIEL GARCÍA MÁRQUEZ · *Bon Voyage, Mr President*
PATRICK MCGRATH · *The Angel*
HERMAN MELVILLE · *Bartleby*
SPIKE MILLIGAN · *Gunner Milligan, 954024*
MICHEL DE MONTAIGNE · *Four Essays*
JAN MORRIS · *From the Four Corners*
JOHN MORTIMER · *Rumpole and the Younger Generation*
R. K. NARAYAN · *Tales from Malgudi*
ANAIS NIN · *A Model*
FRANK O'CONNOR · *The Genius*
GEORGE ORWELL · *Pages from a Scullion's Diary*
CAMILLE PAGLIA · *Sex and Violence, or Nature and Art*
SARA PARETSKY · *A Taste of Life*
EDGAR ALLAN POE · *The Pit and the Pendulum*
MISS READ · *Village Christmas*
JEAN RHYS · *Let Them Call It Jazz*
DAMON RUNYON · *The Snatching of Bookie Bob*
SAKI · *The Secret Sin of Septimus Brope*
WILL SELF · *Scale*
GEORGES SIMENON · *Death of a Nobody*
MURIEL SPARK · *The Portobello Road*
ROBERT LOUIS STEVENSON · *The Pavilion on the Links*
PAUL THEROUX · *Down the Yangtze*
WILLIAM TREVOR · *Matilda's England*
MARK TULLY · *Ram Chander's Story*
JOHN UPDIKE · *Friends from Philadelphia*
EUDORA WELTY · *Why I Live at the P. O.*
EDITH WHARTON · *Madame de Treymes*
OSCAR WILDE · *The Happy Prince*
VIRGINIA WOOLF · *Killing the Angel in the House*